THE WAY TO MIDNIGHT

THE WAY TO MIDNIGHT

Dangerous relationships
don't always look like it...
a true story

ANNA HOUSEGO

1st Edition 2018, paperback.
ISBN: 978-1-925764-52-9
Publishing services by: PublishMyBook.Online

A catalogue record for this book is available from the National Library of Australia.

For Holly and Oliver, who each found their voice.
And for the lost ones who never could.

1

Her thoughts were wild things today, whirling and snarling, rushing away then back. She was a sensible girl, everyone said it, so it was good they didn't know about this bedlam in her head.

The billycan bumped against her bare leg as she jumped from one railway sleeper to the next, the handle loose in her fingers and the tin billy swinging back and forth. Maybe this would be the last time she would see Reg. The last chance for a future.

The previous Sunday in church, while the priest had read Ezekiel's words about tin, silver and other metals being thrown into a furnace, Zillah could swear she had felt a blast of a different kind of heat. "So I will gather you in my anger and in my wrath, and I will lay you there and melt you." Her face had flushed and when Father Hayes looked over, she had stared down at the cushion on the kneeling rail for fear he would see in her face a reflection of thoughts a good Catholic woman should not have.

To settle herself, she'd focused hard on how strange it was that for five centuries human hands had used something that was produced almost at the bottom of her street. Tin was the reason their town was here and had been found in the cassiterite that had at first been easy pickings on the mountain summit and slopes but harder work once that supply had been exhausted, yielding only to open-cut mining and quarrying.

As a child, on one rare occasion when her father had sat by the stove and told them stories about Waratah's early days and his work at the mine, he had talked about how tin would cry. A thin kind of creaking, he said, that the crystals gave off when narrow bars of the metal were bent. While her brothers spent days pounding empty tin cans to see if they could make the sound, she could only wonder what dreadfulness it would take to make rocks shed tears.

The gouged bowl of Mount Bischoff was behind Zillah as she walked out of town towards Magnet Junction on that cold Wednesday morning. It was hard to believe that five thousand people had once lived around here. She would soon turn twenty-three yet she had only ever known the pockmarked timber cottages to house fewer than a thousand locals, and she was far too young to have seen the way miners had swung from ropes to crack ore on the Brown Face, like abseiling into the gaping jaws of hell, her teacher had said.

She was proud it had been one of the richest tin mines in the world, rescuing the entire island from economic ruin and starting a mining frenzy that gripped much of the West Coast mountain country. Great riches had flowed north, turning the backwater of Burnie into a thriving port town and fattening the wallets of merchants and bankers. Further east along the coastline, new wealth had conjured sandstone, metal lacework and civic fountains for the grand city of Launceston. It was true, though, that genteel folk averted their gaze and covered their mouths to prevent coughing fits when forced to venture near the city's edge, where the mining company's smelter stacks punctured the sky.

A seemingly endless supply had been torn from the mountain of tin, yet each time the locomotive pulled away from the station and steamed across the iron bridge in the direction of Burnie, the heart of the mine had grown a little weaker. Nobody believed it would ever end but then, who had imagined the mine would be so badly managed or that there would be a Great Depression?

For Zillah, Waratah was home and she was a native creature curled up in the warmth of routine, held in the predictability of the cold blasts of wind and the rain that fell more days than not; accepting the comfort of friends and families who clung tenaciously to whatever living they could make.

It had never occurred to her that the town might truly be dying. Even Old Rocky, who lived with his pack of dogs in the tin shed near the butcher shop, laughed about the way they always reckoned the undertaker was coming to bury Waratah and never did. She laughed about it, too. She was a Housego, a west coaster, and her family and the town were not going anywhere.

It was 3 April 1935 and while the end of the month would bring the heaviest rains on record, for now the sky was clear. As she followed the metal rails near the final curve before the junction, a lone currawong waited for a warmer sun on a low limb of a nearby tree, its feathers shiny black. Zillah glanced up to see one yellow eye with its dark centre fixed on her. For a long moment she was staring back into inky depths, while all around them stretched a dull sky.

Zillah slowed, almost coming to a halt, feeling the pulse of blood in her veins and the emptiness of the eye exploring her. As she looked back, the blackness at the centre of the eye seemed to fade at first and then grow stronger, no longer nothing but narrowing to a bright pinpoint folding in on itself. It was opening inwards, a tiny portal into what might be an entire world; beckoning, drawing in and pulling her with it. Her shoulders twitched, breaking her gaze, and she turned away. "Just a stupid bird," she muttered, as she hurried off.

Zillah suddenly felt cold and pulled the collar of her brown woollen coat tightly around her neck, cursing the smell of the stale perfume. Did she really need the reminder every time she wore it that the coat was a hand-me-down? It had come from her sister, Isobel, only two years older but a woman who liked to think of herself as the city one in the family after her stint nursing off the island, in Victoria.

She remembered the night Isobel had returned,

how she had brought out the perfume bottle with a flourish, showing off her precious purchase, Evening in Paris. Zillah smiled to herself as she passed Delphin's Paddock, thinking about how fanciful it was; as if a night in France was something her sister would ever be likely to experience.

She looked over her shoulder back down the line but couldn't see Reg. That was good—it gave her time to go to the Kelly house and let Kathleen know she would be a few minutes late for blackberry picking.

Odd, she thought, how the pleasure of knowing she would see him was greater than the sadness of his leaving. Last night he had seemed so resolute as they held hands in the shadows of the railway station; had said he wanted to talk to her about something special. Her boots grew heavy and she slowed, no longer leaping from one railway sleeper to the next but accepting gravel or timber, whatever was rising to meet each footfall. It was hopeless to think they might marry when, after all, she was the problem. Perhaps he had a plan, she comforted herself; a way to stay in touch.

Reginald Sutton, known to all as Reg. She had noticed him from the post office vestibule the first day he arrived in town, a man who was not especially tall but definitely solid, with his biceps a hard lump against each shirtsleeve as he strode away with the mail for the Waratah Hotel.

"He's the reason the Burnie Surf Club's been winning races," Kathleen said with a sense of authority, warming to the subject. "I've read about him in the paper. He's their number one beltman, which means he's their strongest swimmer. The beltman swims out to whoever's in trouble in the surf and saves them," she added in a rush.

Zillah laughed and reminded Kathleen that lifesaving was a team effort and any rescue depended on others paying out a line and reeling in both the beltman and the swimmer in trouble. She loved Kathleen but at times it was obvious that her friend was only eighteen and still had a lot of growing up to do.

She had to admit though, that Kathleen had got something right that day. The barman was a one-off, standing out like the runt in a litter, not especially small but a bundle of spit and determination. He was different from the local men Zillah knew from the district dances. She could see at a glance there was something that set him apart. But the vocabulary she had learned addressed itself to practical matters and not to nuance, so it remained elusive.

She had been seeing Reg for more than a year, not in secret but with enough stealth for it to remain low-key. For months she had been crossing a divide. It had started easily enough, stolen moments with him then slipping back home to return to her chores and family. Back and forth she went. Until it was no longer a line she was crossing but had widened to a river, calm on the surface as she waded over but concealing in its depths dark, slippery beasts that surfaced when she least expected it.

It wasn't as if she would wish for their relationship to have happened any other way over those months of snatching time with him because, she knew, it had been enough to have it for herself. Now it needed to be made different, without someone breaking. How could she manage it?

Each day bent quietly to the next in a rhythm she had come to expect, in a pattern of work and play followed willingly. She was the compliant daughter, the unsurprising one. It had been enough for her, until the question arrived and refused to move out. Now it was growing more insistent. She felt like a door hanging from one hinge, except a door did not know it needed more to hold it. At any moment she might give way with the effort of carrying the question that she dared not voice. What about me?

It was nearly 11 am when Zillah circled the goods sheds where the narrow gauge line ended the struggle of its zigzag journey up from the nearby silver mine at Magnet, coming to a T-junction with the branch line she had been walking on. From here the steel rails from Waratah slithered east about fifteen miles to Guildford Junction and the Emu Bay Railway Company's main line.

For years, Guildford had been the only threshold to the world, a place to pause and relinquish the moment of arriving before plunging onwards with the journey. The steam train took on water while passengers hurried into the warmth of the station bar for a home-cooked meal or a beer, before continuing north to Burnie and its safe harbour or south to West Coast mining towns and the craggy peaks that kept them apart.

Zillah was old enough to remember when life had begun to change, how men made jobless by the Depression had flayed rainforest trees and the scrub of wet gullies with axes, picks and shovels, forcing a path for the narrow road away from town. These days, her family and many other locals took the faster motor car service for shopping trips or visits to Burnie.

She swung left, up the rise where a few simple fettlers' cottages had been built above the racket of shunting trains and clanging wagons. From here, she turned around to look back, and caught a glimpse of the roof of her house near the edge of town.

At the gate she called out to Kathleen, who came straight out, wiping her hands on an apron.

"Be with you in a minute, I've just got to make my sandwich," Kathleen said, tugging at the ties on the back of her apron.

"That's okay. I've got to catch up with Reg for a bit, anyway. I might leave my things here, though."

Zillah swung the billycan with the lunch over the fence to Kathleen, followed by the empty bucket for blackberries.

"Don't be long, Zillah. I don't want to be hanging around here waiting." Kathleen scowled but who could be cross with this girl?

Zillah gave a grin and waved one hand in her friend's direction. As she stepped away she called out: "See you soon".

Kathleen shrugged her shoulders and gave a wry smile, turning away with the notion that it was odd for her friend to be meeting Reg so early in the day. The thought vanished as she rushed back inside to beat her brother to the last of the fish paste for her sandwich, not bothering to see which way Zillah had gone.

2

Everything about hockey suited Zillah. Breathless running and diving, the crack of the stick on the ball, the thrill of winging a shot past the goalie, the flying chatter with the other Centrals girls while they decorated the hall for fundraising dances. She loved it all, including the painstaking task of cleaning her boots, digging out the glass-hard mud caked on the stops.

From the sports oval where they played, on a rise above the river and the mine dam, she could see the landscape of her life. The stately Athenaeum Hall and its soaring single gable, the courtroom and the council chambers, the modest hospital, were all on this side of the valley gash. The railway station and locomotive sheds overlooked the valley mouth, and lining the other side were the shops, post office and two hotels. Together, they drew the town in tight against the frontier of dense, wet forests that stretched deep into the gorge below where, confined no more, they pushed out with all their vigour to rows of mountains and the horizon.

The river was a giant question mark, flowing straight and narrow where it was parallel to Smith Street, below the oval, then curling behind the mine manager's house and under the iron railway bridge. There, in the centre of town, it dropped out of sight over a sharp, rocky lip.

In an instant, it was a foaming, thundering beast that rushed 300 feet straight down to slam the valley floor. Often in winter when it flooded, a blunt outcrop just below the lip split the waterfall in two and it roared down the valley in double glory.

The town sprawled across a plateau 2000 feet above sea level, exposing it to winds from every direction. Southerlies and south-westerlies blasted in with hail and snow, leaving icicles hanging more than three feet long from the timber aqueduct that carried water to the mine. Restless north-westerlies drove heavy rains that pounded the town, showing no mercy for days on end. The easterlies were warmer but blanketed homes with misty rain, the damp slipping under doors, through cracks and down chimneys to lodge in bedding and clothes. Mould grew on shoes, in the back of cupboards and under mattresses not turned every week.

Threading through the town from the top of the waterfall and around the valley mouth, the mine's rail tracks and powerlines ran in several directions, as though a crazed spider had been spinning in steel. They connected sheds to the treatment plant and the calciner, defying gravity on opposite slopes of Happy Valley, before searching out the mountain.

The old-timers had told Zillah about the calciner furnace spitting out sour fumes of sulphur that, when the wind blew towards town, hid in nasal cavities and triggered nosebleeds for anyone caught in their path. Even after the smell had dispersed, they said, fine particles caught in the lungs of asthmatics and those prone to bronchitis and the hawking and spitting had been terrible to hear.

These days the sulphur fumes were blasted with water and the lethal mix flushed into the river. Despite the absence of vapour nothing had dared grow back in the afflicted soil around the calciner, where stands of sassafras, leatherwood, myrtles and soaring, thick-trunked ferns had once jostled for sunlight. The stain spread downstream for about fifteen miles, pouring through the valley in a bubbling river of acid. Its sulphur-saturated water killed off slick brown trout and giant freshwater lobsters that were the largest of their kind in the world, some of them three decades old.

The town had been named for its primitive waratah flowers, which grew in clusters on tall shrubs with stiff, glossy leaves. The arrival of the postbox-red flowers, each about the size of a small hand with delicate, tube-like tendrils curling in from the base like slender fingers cupping the air, set the local children to shrieking and writing letters to Santa because it meant that Christmas was close.

Once, Zillah had stumbled across a rare white waratah when she and some friends, bored with the inter-town rivalry of athletics and chopping competitions at the annual Muddy Creek district miners' picnic, had gone exploring. Too young to spend time admiring the strength of the young men, their muscles straining through singlets as they swung axes, she and the other girls had left the busy clearing and pushed through low scrub in search of adventure. Within minutes they were thrashing through a tight stand of tea-trees that lay in the opposite direction to the easier bush. This spared them any sightings of furtive couples, the cause of forced weddings that inevitably followed what locals had dubbed the Shotgun Carnival.

The girls had emerged into open eucalypt forest and were brushing prickly leaves from their faces and necks when Zillah spotted the lone shrub. As she touched the white waratahs with their yellow blush, the waxy blooms seemed foreign, like they should not be there at all, and it felt wrong to pick them so she told the others to let them be. The astonishing find was never shared with the adults as it had been over-shadowed by the panic of their families when they almost missed the train home.

It was said the *Telopea truncata* had been growing in ancient times and Zillah liked to think the special white ones were there when, who knows, Australia might have been joined to Antarctica. She had read about the possibility of a supercontinent in a book she'd borrowed from the library, and made the mistake of saying so as the family sat around scraping thick gravy and mashed spuds off their plates.

Her father had snorted so hard that brown spots of gravy sprayed onto the faded tablecloth and his knife and fork jerked up.

"Why would you believe such a stupid thing?" He was wild-eyed and they all went quiet.

"It's a furphy, and the Great War is all the proof we need that you can't trust the Germans, let alone German science men and their twisted way of looking at the world."

Everyone looked down at their plates and waited for the storm to pass. They knew better than to attempt to argue, which had the same effect as setting a match to a Catherine wheel on bonfire night but without the fun.

Bill took their silence as agreement and went back to wrestling thick slices of mutton into his mouth. As far as he was concerned, that was the end of the matter. He wasn't to know that his dismissal of the German meteorologist's theory had come too late.

The idea had already heated Zillah's imagination and she pictured powerful opposing forces stretching the bottom half of the globe. She saw a vast southern land straining and cracking, Antarctica snapping away in one direction and Australia in the other, with her upside-down triangle of an island the last piece to be ripped away. She didn't need her father to agree. The proof for her was the map showing Tasmania hanging like an afterthought off the south-eastern tip of the mainland.

Up on the rise at the sportsground, where Zillah stood ready to strap on her shin pads, the mountain appeared at its broadest, a giant animal spread low on its haunches yet watchful. Its scarred purple face turned towards the scattered rows of cottages and the only road out of town.

She was filling in as goalie today so when she bent down to fit the leather pads she double-checked the buckles to make sure they were tight. What was the point of turning nineteen a few weeks ago, she thought, if she was no closer to having a life she could call her own. Some of her school friends were already married, one with a baby on the way, yet she had no boyfriend and not much chance of finding one.

With tin prices plummeting, the Mount Bischoff Mining Company had switched to the tributer system, which left miners scratching for tin in their own small operations around the mountain and working long hours for little reward. Many of the young men left when they became old enough to work.

If that wasn't bad enough, she only had to see the line-up at local football matches or the empty pews at St Joseph's to know that Catholic men were outnumbered by about three to one. She was not inclined to worry about things but it was hard to see what her future might hold.

Her name was Hebrew for "shadow". While it meant shadow of darkness, her nature leaned more to sun and light. She was a young girl when she found her namesake in the Old Testament, appearing as one of the two wives of Lamech—and one of the most important women in the Bible. The biblical Zillah had birthed a son and the beginnings of civilisation, for it was her son, Tubal-cain, who had established the ancient crafts of metalsmiths and ironmaking. The biblical version, Zillah decided years later, had left the kind of legacy that was laughable for a mining town woman.

It had been a shock when, at almost nine years old and taking instruction from Father Hayes before her confirmation, Zillah had discovered there was more to the story. Her biblical counterpart had been one of the Cainites, descended from the brother who was murderer and sinner and not from the saint, Abel. "The seed of Satan," Father Hayes called Cain. "The covetous and not the righteous," he intoned to the children, warming to the cautionary tale of how the perils of sin would lead to their undoing, just as Cain had been cursed by God and expelled from the paradise of Eden.

As the young girl listened to the priest speaking with such conviction, her name became a burden almost too great to bear, carrying the great Catholic weight of guilt and the dreadful certainty of getting things wrong. Later, when she asked her mother why she had chosen it, Alice said she had always liked it for its musical sound and that made Zillah feel happier, though she never felt the same about it. From then on her name was more like stone than song as it came from the mouths of others.

A newspaper would, too late, describe the grown-up Zillah as one of the most attractive girls in the district but it was not a description she could embrace. Her mother called her a livewire, which was closer to the truth of how she saw herself.

As for her looks, she tolerated the short brown bob of her hair, the fringe mostly pinned to one side to keep it out of her eyes. But when she looked in the dressing-table mirror, the effect of her long limbs was lanky rather than womanly and her dresses hung straight without the shapely effect she secretly sought.

The one photo of herself she liked was in a heavy gilt frame hanging in the front room, used only when special visitors came. Her mother had saved money for family portraits by Winters Studio on one of their trips to West Coast towns. It was taken when she was fifteen and she had sat on a straight-backed chair in her lace-collared dress. The black and white image had been hand-coloured by the photographic studio so the lace looked creamy and the dress a much richer brown than in real life. Her youngest sister had sat on her lap. Jean, barely a toddler then, her knitted dress and jacket bulky over a cloth nappy, her face unhappy at the strangeness of the photographer and the need to sit still. Zillah liked the way, above the baby's head, her own oval face turned slightly left, facing the camera with a softness she did not see in the mirror. It grew more appealing with each passing year that she studied the picture. Perhaps in time the tomboy would be willing to hand over to the woman.

"Zillah, Zillah, get a move on!"

Her Centrals teammates were waving frantically and she ran over to join them, laughing and flinging an arm around her friend Winnie while they all shouted a rousing chant, crossed sticks and hoped for another win against Philippians.

ERIC WAS WAITING FOR her when she got home. At twenty-five and always conscious of being the eldest brother, he found it just as easy as the others to get caught up in Zillah's exuberance or be amused by her sense of the ridiculous, but he was usually the first to get serious with her.

"The boys and I have been talking," he said, without waiting for her to change out of her dirt-spattered hockey shift. She imagined him bailing up Bill, a year younger than him and a miner like their dad, and Jack, at eighteen the most recent one to go out to work.

"We know you'd like to be earning, which would likely mean leaving here. So we had a talk with Mum and she's agreed. The boys and 1 will all put in a bit of money and pay you every fortnight so you can stay home and help around here."

This was the first she'd heard of it and she wanted to look Eric in the eye but found she couldn't. Instead, she studied the scuffed pattern on the kitchen mat and wondered why she didn't feel more grateful. Mother's little helper, she thought, but didn't say it aloud.

"Thanks, that's good of you," she managed.

Eric waited a moment but when he realised her silence was the end of it, he went outside to take a turn with the block-buster, lining it up with the grain as he worked with the momentum from each downward swing to split sawed rounds of a fallen eucalypt into pieces of firewood.

Thirteen-year-old Cyril came in the back door, causing a commotion when he stuck out his boot and tripped their youngest brother, Phil, born only a year later, causing him to knock his shoulder hard on the architrave.

When Isobel got back from her shift at the hospital about an hour later, Zillah was carrying in wood to build up the fire in the stove while her mother sliced cubes of lamb for an Irish stew.

"So the boys are paying you to stay home? Aren't you the lucky one," Isobel said.

Zillah ignored her sister, though she wanted to snap back that luck was something unexpected to lift you out of your circumstances or save you when all was lost, not a tether with one end around your ankle and the other tied to the leg of a kitchen table. The arrangement gave her an independent income and, truth be told, she welcomed that, but it was hard to see it as such good fortune.

"It's still work, Isobel, even if I wear an apron instead of a fancy uniform!"

The next day, she went looking for the last of the season's gooseberries, on the low bushes growing haphazardly in what had once been a well-tended yard not far from her home but now a vacant paddock. As she crouched to slide under the bottom strand of fencing wire, she remembered standing there with Isobel and Phil only a few years ago, thinking how strange it was to see a house cut in half.

It had taken the men most of the day, grunting and swearing, to jack each section up and manoeuvre one then the other onto separate truck beds. As the day wore on, more onlookers joined them and by late afternoon, a large group had gathered, laughing and chatting as though they were at a carnival. By the time the two loads pulled slowly away towards Burnie, the mood had shifted. The crowd separated to stand on either side of the road, their faces solemn as they watched the trucks leave.

As the months had gone by other houses had been dismantled, the timber stacked neatly and taken to build homes on farms and in the growing suburbs rising from the hills around Burnie or recycled for sheds and warehouses. After the mine's open-cut operation closed in 1929, only folks with their feet planted in local soil had stayed on.

Zillah squeezed the flesh from the plumpest gooseberries, flicking it onto the ground then chewing the tart green skins, enjoying the way they set her teeth on edge. She picked some for a pie and thought of waiting around to see if Kathleen was on her way home from the shops but changed her mind and went home.

She heard them arguing before she reached the back door and her body stiffened, instinctively bracing for what might be a passing squall of reproach or a full-blown storm that might not blow itself out for an hour or more. What would it be this time? Probably her father angry again because her mother had dared chat to Mr Richardson over the neighbour's front fence. As she unlaced her boots it occurred to Zillah that the arguing was much more frequent lately and so were the urgent conversations she sometimes overheard between her father and Eric.

The night before, she had come in quietly after visiting Kathleen and caught them swearing about a hike in the price the Mount Bischoff company was charging to crush the tributers' ore. More than 170 local men fossicked on any sites they could to retrieve tin from tailings or attack ore that sometimes took months to break before it could be transported to the mill for crushing. The costs did not end there, and if the ore contained pyrite then it had to go to the roasting plant for treatment. All this was but a fraction of the mine's output in its heyday, now stripped to its bare bones for a total of about 450 tons—on the backs of men who strained for a pittance while the Mount Bischoff company held out its hand for a profit.

She could still hear their tense voices when she'd gone to bed, complaining about how, after they bagged their tin, it was three pounds a ton for the train to Burnie. "Then there's the cost of the insurance and the hospital subscription and the prices they keep pushing up for explosives and tools." Eric was almost spitting out the words.

The mine sheds, the stamper batteries thumping out the regular beat of a mechanical heart alongside Main Street, the reservoir for the power station, the loco hauling ore trucks, rotting timber falling downhill from the original water-run mill that once perched at the top of the falls, erosion in the valley —these were all evidence of the way the Mount Bischoff company had moulded the place.

Zillah had grown up with the mining company's fingerprints on every part of life, yet she was the fish that makes no distinction between its gills and water. She had no inkling of the invisible presence in marital beds, at family gatherings, in stunted hopes or heated livers. The rising fortunes of the company had brought the town into fullness of life with easy wealth on the mountain surface and below in seams and fissures but now its falling fortunes were taking it under.

It was beyond her, captured as she was in the business of getting a foothold in adult life, to grasp how badly the mine had been managed in the rush for profits and the way her family and neighbours were paying the price.

Lying in bed, it all sounded difficult and complicated and she came to the conclusion that she did not understand the issues at all but that was okay because she was not the one who needed to. Her father's growl had been the last thing she heard as she dozed off: "We're like a wallaby with its foot caught in a snare, bloody oath we are."

As she opened the kitchen door, she smelled the buttery pastry on the beef pasties before she saw them cooling, and just for a moment was glad her mother had made her dig up, peel and chop the swedes and potatoes before she'd left that morning.

"I don't bloody care who he is," Bill's voice punched at the air. "No wife of mine is gonna be talking to any fella on her own."

His bony frame curved forward a little, bent from the years in the mine, and now that he spent most days stooped over a pan sluicing tin from the tailings at his workings there seemed no reason to bother drawing himself upright. Taller than Bill at his full height, Alice was at the crockery cupboard with her feet planted apart, one hand holding a stack of plates with tiny blue and yellow flowers on the rim disappearing into the folds of her waist, and the other braced on a shelf.

She was stern and solid, from good farming stock on the dairy plains out the back of Westbury where the Great Western Tiers held back the horizon. She had never expected to be raising children in a mining town, let alone one where the clothes always smelled of wood smoke because she was forever drying them in front of the fire while sheets of rain stung the windows and walls. She had been born after the one who died and given the same name, marking her out to carry the dead one's destiny and, in time, to fill her arms with the burden of her own children. It had been a sign, the year she came squawking into the world in the shanty at the foot of Quamby Bluff, that the bees had deserted their hives and taken with them all the sweetness of their honey.

Her husband's contorted face in front of her was making her head spin. Maybe if she had been blessed with a sense of humour like Zillah's, she could laugh right now. What was it the Launceston *Examiner* had printed when she married Bill? Oh yes: "We wish them a pleasant trip o'er the troublous waves of life." Well, there had been plenty of trouble and not much that was pleasant.

The old questions were agitating again. She had asked them many times without getting a single answer that made it worth the way they brought her low, left her circling all the days she could never take back. What if she had not been sent to live here with her aunt and uncle, taking up the job as a cook? What if she'd stayed in the family home near the bluff? If she had not caught the eye of the man so much older than her?

So much that could have swung another way, she thought. It was madness to keep going over it. After all, she was Irish. She was Paddy Hartnett's daughter and she came from a long line of survivors, people who fought to keep their land and when that was taken, fought to keep their food. And when the potato famine wiped that out, they fought with all they had left to keep their Roman Catholic beliefs and here, on the other side of the world, to keep their Irish roots close by.

Her ancestors in County Limerick had known about holding true to a path and with starvation all around in the Great Famine, they had refused to become "soupers" and renounce their faith for some British crumbs and a Protestant prayer book. Laws had wiped out their right to worship and the blood-hounds had hunted down their priests, but they had never stopped believing. They'd been banned from speaking their language but they had done it all the more in their own home or their neighbours' houses. When they'd been prevented from educating their children, they had helped find houses, barns or other secret places where they did it anyway.

Famine. Now that could defeat you. War. Oh yes, it could take you down, like her darling brothers Denny and John, left on the wire in France all those years ago. Yes, she reminded herself, the trick was to hold on and hold out, hoping for a sliver of grace, praying for your children to grow strong, get an education and have a better life.

She didn't see herself as a hard-hearted woman and there had been a time when she'd felt sorry for Bill. It wasn't as though life had been easy for him, and when she met him, the pain of his father dying when he'd been fifteen years old was still in his eyes. It had been months before he told her that consumption had not only taken his father but had orphaned him and his fourteen siblings. Their mother had died the year before, the sheets flooded with bright red blood when the placenta refused to budge after childbirth.

Alice had often wondered if Bill's temper and his short fuse had been a product of a young boy's sense of a cruel world and his panic about making a way on his own. It wasn't a conversation her husband would ever entertain and in any case, he was not one for talking.

Lord knows, life had been hard with him so difficult and the eight kids coming almost year after year, the pattern broken only by the three miscarriages. She had first seen Bill at the end of a pew at St Joseph's, she just shy of twenty-two and him a good ten years older. She was a god-fearing woman but these days she didn't have much time for St Joseph, patron saint of the workers or at least the working man. He had not, in her experience, kept much of an eye on the endless grind of the wives.

"Am I supposed to ignore our neighbour, when all he's done is happen to be on his verandah when I go past?"

She hurled the words at him and as she did, Bill's arms went rigid beside his body and his hands tightened, the fingers locked hard.

"You'll do as I say," he hollered back, one fist raised.

Zillah saw it and took a step forward, closer to her mother. The room closed in to the small triangle of space between the three of them. Her father was shaking, his cheeks flushed red.

"You're just a jealous old coot who's never happy about anything." It came out of Alice's mouth steady, matter of fact. She was unexpectedly calm now and for a moment the lack of fight within caught her off-guard. Bill saw it too and stopped shouting.

She had doggedly followed the one path, the right path, for years, and finally there was nothing willing her on for the sake of the marriage or the thin trickle of money. It was clear now, all of it. She was looking at him and what she saw was not his sunken face but the foolish dreams from long ago, and there was no escaping it—her hopes were completely worn out, including the final threadbare one of a truce.

"From tomorrow, Bill, you stay down at the camp. You're no longer sleeping here or living here. If you want to come for the roast on Sundays, that's your business."

Zillah was struggling to get her bearings. This was not how it usually went and she turned away from the blank map of her mother to look for familiar signs in her dad. He seemed frozen and for an awful moment she thought he'd stopped breathing, till she noticed a faint tic at the base of his neck.

When he eventually sucked in air to speak, he surprised even himself. "I'll gladly take my things when I go down the valley tomorrow and I'll stay there, where at least I won't have to bloody well listen to you harping."

The pause that stretched out, ragged across the room, was broken when six-year-old Jean burst in from playing with friends after school. Zillah hugged her before starting their favourite tickling game, the girls wriggling and giggling together. As Zillah continued to keep Jean distracted, she flicked an occasional glance at her parents. Her father sank into the chair near the stove, elbows on the wooden arms and an out-of-date newspaper in front of his face. Her mother continued setting the table. When the others straggled in from work and play, Zillah was glad to call them in to the usual bump and bustle of their evening meal.

Nothing more was said and Zillah knew that, after all the shouting that had come before, it was done. She had a queer feeling, sitting with the others around the table, as though a big old stringybark had fallen somewhere out there in the shadowy tangle of bush and she was the only one to feel the ground tremble.

3

Zillah tried not to look in his direction as she quick-stepped up and down the hall on the floor she and her friends had waxed only hours earlier, but whenever she snatched a quick glance he was looking back. The green balloons and crepe paper streamers surrounding the stage where the band played and the fern fronds lining the hall gave a nod to St Patrick's Day at one of the most popular balls of the year.

She'd decided that green was not her best colour and instead wore pink crepe de chine. As she danced with Maggie past the group of men hovering at the back of the hall where they could easily duck out for beer, she was sorry for a moment it was the empire-waisted dress because although it was floor-length, in hindsight it was a little too girlish for a twenty-two year old.

Reg was happy to be near the keg, despite serving ale all afternoon at the Waratah Hotel. He'd only been in town for a couple of weeks but some of the local lads knew about his form on the football field and had been quick to recruit him to play for Waratah in the upcoming season.

Amid the backslapping of the men in the semi-darkness near the hall's main exit, it turned out they had seen the recent *North-Western Advocate* story on his win in the Beach to Beach swim. He hardly thought of it as a triumph when he'd been the only one to make it past the halfway mark but the others were impressed.

"Yeah," one of them said, "that's what we need, a tough bugger like you as centre half forward to flatten those bloody Rovers like you did the breakers at West Beach."

When the band stopped for the interval, he followed the others up the stairs and behind the stage to the supper room, where trestle tables were choked with trays of sandwiches and egg and bacon pies, as well as plates of delicate butterfly cakes, jelly-coated snowballs dusted with shredded coconut, sponge cakes, lamingtons and raspberry slice. At the far end was a small table with cups and milk jugs. His luck was in, he thought, when he saw she was there and pouring tea from a huge teapot. Better still, he could get a good look at her because all her attention was on balancing the weight of the pot with the main handle while lowering and raising it with the small handle near the lid. The entire action reminded him of a bird dipping to drink at a waterhole as she repeated the motion for each teacup that was presented for filling.

He ate a couple of sandwiches and a pie without really tasting them while he waited till the queue dwindled. Although what he badly needed was another beer, he went over with a cup and saucer and introduced himself, leaning forward a little to disguise the fact that at nearly five foot nine he was much taller than her.

Zillah looked up into hazel eyes that were oddly intense for such a gentle colour and a face that, were it not for the eyes, you would call perfectly handsome. As he bent for her to pour, she looked over his shoulder at her mother, glad to see Alice was facing the door and had been the unfortunate target for a conversation with Mrs Mulcahy, who would offer no reprieve until the band started up again.

"Going down to Magnet next Friday for the dance?" he asked. His hair, thick and brown, was short at the sides and swept back evenly off his forehead to lie over the crown, yet she saw no sign of the oily pomade the other men combed through theirs to keep it in place.

"I haven't been down there before and it'd be good to know someone who's going," he added.

Zillah couldn't remember ever seeing any man around Waratah with a heart-shaped mouth. *Go easy, don't be too friendly*, she thought, then immediately ignored her own advice and gave him a warm, wide smile.

"Yes, I am. You can walk along with us if you like. We usually leave from the top pub about seven. They let us change down there in the hall beforehand and you'll need a lamp." She paused and tilted her head. "You might need to practise some dancing first, though."

He grinned. *Cheeky sort*, he thought. He'd show her. He thanked her and went back to the keg, content to know he would only have to wait a week.

ON THE FRIDAY NIGHT after lock-up, Reg helped the other barman clean up then got his bag and a borrowed lantern and went up to the Bischoff Hotel. Zillah was there on the footpath with half-a-dozen men and women in their early twenties. They waited for the last few stragglers and set off towards the mountain, soon veering left away from the mine workings. They threaded down the foothills of West Bischoff and into dense rainforest and a thick gloom that dampened the lights they carried to a feeble glow.

Most of the group had taken the Tinstone Creek track before and as they picked their way down the steep early section, some began singing, almost yelling as they warmed up. "That's why I'm yearning, just to be returning, along the road to Gundagai, yai yai."

Reg, who was behind two men taking the lead, wondered how it would be on the stiff climb back after a few hours' drinking and was pleased when the track levelled out to skirt the base of surrounding hills. Unlike the ten-mile railway line renowned for turning on itself through 197 corners as it nosed through the hills on the other side of town, this was a direct route closer to half that distance.

About an hour later, their excited chatter could be heard in cottages clustered along the railway line as they crossed the footbridge over Magnet Creek and arrived in the hush of the settlement. They were the first at the hall. The smell of kerosene, woodchips and candle scrapings used to polish the myrtle boards to a warm glow hit them as they piled in the door, shedding muddy boots and laughing about who would be the first one to go over on the slippery floor.

The men stayed at the back of the hall and laced on dancing shoes buffed to a high shine while the women peeled away to the ladies toilet. They sloughed off drab outer layers of coats and workaday skirts to wriggle into brightly coloured dance dresses and strappy heels.

Zillah slipped on a deep blue dress with a swirling skirt well above her ankles, a bodice gathered gently to show off the bust, and a keyhole neckline finished with a flattering soft bow. The dress felt more awkward than she'd expected, not so much because she'd taken advantage of Isobel staying the weekend at Burnie to sneak the dress from her wardrobe but, rather, it was a bit sophisticated and maybe she wouldn't be able to carry it off.

She and her friends entered the main hall where local dancers were beginning to fill the space and in the fuss of greeting familiar faces, she failed to register Reg staring in her direction. The hall could take about two hundred, not counting the kids dashing about on the fringes of the dance floor or the five or so prams pushed into the darkest corner, and it was close to capacity.

Young mothers joined the matrons sitting on narrow wooden benches against the walls as the four-piece band warmed up but the moment the first tune began, they sprang up, leaving the older women to their gossiping. They were there to snatch their share of fun, God knows there was little enough of it, and were off their seats and onto the floor as the first wheezing notes flew from the accordion.

The women mostly danced with each other, not willing to waste a single chord. Waiting out on the hillside were the sticky mud, smoky chimneys and dinners to cook but for now, they wore lipstick, heels and carefully curled hair and be damned if they would sit about waiting for the men to get enough beer into them to take to the floor.

As the evening progressed, Zillah strained to act normally. Unlike the usual laughter and lightness of dancing with her girlfriends or the boys from her school days, she was aware she was distracted. "Oh Lordy, get your act together," she whispered to herself.

Reg was on the other side of the hall, dancing with a girl who worked in the draper's shop at Waratah, then he disappeared for a set before returning to sashay around the floor with another local girl. Zillah was sitting this one out and watched them, crestfallen, as they swept through the crowd of dancers.

"Cheer up," Kathleen said, leaning into her shoulder. "You know he's a Proddie and nothing could come of it anyway. Mary said last week that Father Hayes showed up out of the blue while her dad was away and told her mum they were all bastards because she's not a Catholic, even though the old man goes to St Joseph's. Mary said her mum was really upset and crying after."

Zillah didn't quite catch the last bit, or at least she didn't have a chance to think about what Kathleen had said, because at that moment the band stopped briefly for the master of ceremonies to call the next dance and in the lull, Reg was in front of her.

"Care to give it a go?"

He seemed much more shy up close and she could smell beer on his breath as she stood to follow him into the centre of the couples gathered on the floor. When he turned to face her, raising his right hand to take her fingers in the dance hold, she dared not meet his eyes and instead focused on the top button of his shirt to steady herself and disguise a swift tremor.

He held her lightly at first and she was the one clumsy on the corner turns in the slow-slow-quick-quick of the foxtrot, followed by the elegant Pride of Erin. "My favourite," was all she could manage by way of polite conversation. As she stepped forward then back, she relaxed a little under the shelter of his arm, which reached a comfortable height above her shoulders. He said nothing so she tried again to get some talk happening.

"How are you settling in?"

He almost didn't hear her question. It was taking all his concentration to make sure he didn't dance too close as she spun back towards him from the turns. He was battling to keep his touch light as their hands met for him to guide her under his left arm and back to the start of the sequence.

"Yair good. Being in the footy club helps and I still go to Burnie when it's my turn to run the training sessions at the surf club."

That was all he said so she was surprised to find her heart floating up to her throat. She matched his pace through the round but as they advanced forward three steps, facing in the same direction with him behind her shoulder, she closed her eyes for a brief moment, puzzled by the unexpected feeling of wanting to cry but not risking any tears.

After supper, when he returned to get her for the waltz, he was more certain when he clasped her fingers. He guided her around the hall with a firm pressure on her raised hand and she could feel his weight shift to keep time for each step as they circled down the hall. As they came out of the corner near the prams, she felt his other hand slide down from below her shoulder blades to just above the curve of her waist, drawing her a fraction closer so they seemed to dance as one. She settled into letting him lead, the faces around her fading as she waltzed in a pattern he made their own.

When the band stopped for a break, she was happy to sit with her friends, buoyed by the joy of the night, while he slipped out of the hall to join some of the Magnet men in sharing 'dad's crockery', as the local kids called the bottles of ale brought in specially on the train that day. Midnight came fast and soon the musicians were packing away their instruments while the locals hugged goodnight and went home, leaving the Waratah mob to change back into muddy boots and walking clothes.

As they left the settlement, a frog beat of banjo calls bounced off the stillness of the night, fading as the group left behind the damp, soft banks of the creek where the pobblebonks had dug in. The walkers were a tight group at first and their combined lanterns threw out a soft ball of light into the blackness. Soon their energy flagged and they straggled up the track, their lights breaking away into small bursts of yellow that let in the night.

After about a mile, Reg saw Zillah had dropped back towards the rear and he slowed to walk beside her, lifting his lantern in front so they could see the rough surface of the track. Her friends took the hint and stepped up their pace to leave a gap. He was keen to find out what she knew about him but the late hour and the effects of the beer were not helping smooth the lumps in his conversation.

"Get to Burnie much?"

No, she rarely went as most of their shopping was done locally or delivered on the bus.

"You and your family do much reading?"

Christ, he was making a mess of this, as usual. What a stupid damn question when he wasn't the slightest bit interested in what books she might have read. What he really needed to ask was, "Do you or your parents, your brothers and sisters check the daily paper?" But he had to tap-dance around it a bit; it would seem strange if he asked her outright.

He and his brothers Owen and Horrie had been given their fair share of mentions in court reports in recent years. He wasn't so much bothered by the prospect of her knowing about his fight at Ulverstone a few years back—after all, he'd drawn blood on the other two men in the long scuffle and they'd all carried more dirt than bruises. And the speeding fine and the other one for drinking at a pub after six o'clock were not cause for concern.

As for the drunk and disorderly incident, that night had been a real mess and Horrie had been lucky not to go to gaol after punching the copper who was trying to take him to the lock-up. They'd been letting off steam on election night in '31, after Scullin got voted out as Prime Minister. James Scullin might've been a teetotaler but at least he'd been a Labor man, and he'd done the hard yards as a grocer before he got into Parliament. The new fellow, Lyons, hailed from up the road, from Devonport, but what did a school-teacher know about how hard it was to get a bloody job? And he'd betrayed his own party, defecting to hold hands with the Nationalists and form the new United Australia Party. It had been enough to drive anyone to drink.

Then there was Doris. It had only been a couple of months since she'd died. She'd been married and living in Melbourne by then, and it was true they had hardly seen her in recent years but she was their eldest sister just the same. And hell, he lamented, thirty had been way too young for a life to end, with her leaving behind the baby girl and all. Seemed like it got harder not easier to pick yourself up after getting knocked down.

He became aware that Zillah was waiting for him to speak and he struggled out something about how she was obviously a keen reader. She bent her head to the right and smiled at him, her face open. "You don't need to sound so surprised. We're not all country bumpkins around here," she laughed.

"Oh I don't know. There's a few I see in the bar who could do with some sandpaper to take off the rough edges," he parried back.

Instead of circling around, what he really wanted to be sure about was that she hadn't heard how he and Owen had gone to that North Terrace house late in 1930, trying to catch a couple of fowls. It had been a spur of the moment thing and pretty daft to boot, as the house was only a couple of streets away from theirs. The chooks had set up a terrible racket and the owner and his neighbour had caught them in the act.

Within half an hour they'd been arrested but they had done the right thing and pleaded guilty. Trouble was, the damn newspaper had printed what Owen had blurted out to the constable. He really hoped Zillah hadn't read that—such shame for his poor mum— about how they'd gone to the house to steal food because they were hungry. It made them sound like a pack of starving mongrels. There were other things that had been printed, too, but they had come later and he didn't dare think about what had happened or how much she might judge him for it all.

His mind was going crazy with the sudden rush of memories but his voice came out unexpectedly even; he heard it go threading through the ease of her friendly chatter. As they walked in their small pool of light, they found their way to a shared interest in sport. Her tastes went to hockey and badminton, about which he knew next to nothing, but thankfully she was a keen football fan and well-schooled in the sport by her brothers. By the time they started up the steep hill towards the mountain, the others were joining the conversation and he'd satisfied himself that she wasn't much interested in matters outside the town and he would have to take his chances with her family.

They got back to Waratah well past the traditional dipping of lights that signalled five minutes to shut-down at the power station below, in Ringtail Gully. The operator who switched on the turbines to start the town's hydro-electricity service at four o'clock every afternoon had finished his shift and negotiated the narrow path up the gully before midnight, disturbing possums and tiger quolls with his carbide lamp, and was already asleep in his warm bed. Near the pubs and the post office, the weary dancers separated and headed home in different directions for a few hours' sleep before church bells started ringing and mothers began demanding they do chores.

At her house, Zillah slipped in the door, her feet so light she seemed to pass above the squeaky floorboards near the back porch. She was so caught in the memory of the way her skin had hummed when he touched her that she almost forgot the big wooden clock. She doubled back to the mantelpiece and opened the glass door, delicately feeling behind the pendulum to remove the wad of cotton wool she had wedged behind the striker to prevent it boom-ing on the hour and half-hour. She smiled as she did it, enjoying the satisfaction of a rare opportunity to outwit her mother.

In the bedroom, she slipped out of her clothes and left them on the floor before scooting under the blankets and pulling them up tight to her ears. She hugged her knees against her chest to gather up body heat against the chill of the bed. She lay there running through the loop of memories, dancing with Reg again and again, fighting the urge for sleep until it was almost dawn.

A couple of hours later, as the household woke, she dressed and got ready to help with breakfast, surprised that her system was still charged with energy and she was not the slightest bit exhausted. As she stepped into the kitchen, Alice was slicing bread for toast and glanced up. Zillah was conscious that she had changed in some way since leaving for the dance and was uncertain what her mother might see.

"A good night?"

"Yes, it was fun, Mum. They had a good crowd and turned on a big supper. The Bonneys won the chocolate waltz, as usual. Oh, and I hear a couple more families are leaving in the next month."

The last tidbit was designed to derail her mother's questioning but failed to deter her.

"Didn't hear you come in. Was it late?"

"Not especially, Mum. Thought I might weed around the foxgloves after breakfast."

This time her mother took the bait and the conversation drifted to the tasks waiting to be done in the narrow strip of garden along the front fence.

AFTER THE DANCE THERE was no particular decision or discussion between Reg and Zillah about what the arrangement might be. They began stepping out together every chance they could, often in a group but now and then just the two of them, and on those occasions they were discreet. They fell into a rhythm of occasional walks at twilight after his bar shift ended, playing in the euchre tournaments, dancing, sitting near each other at brass band competitions and meeting at fundraising fairs or film nights.

All winter she watched him on the footy field on Saturdays, pleased when he wasn't playing against her brother Bill's Bischoff team and she didn't have to share her allegiances. She was careful afterwards not to hang around in case her brothers saw her talking to Reg and, for his part, he was grateful he got to spend time with her and had no desire to break the spell, brushing off his mates when they tried to tease him about having a girl.

Summer came and with it an uncharacteristic dry spell that crackled through the day, baking puddles to a crust then sucking greedily on the dam in the town and the reservoir a mile away until both were acres of mudflats. At the beginning of March, without water to run the hydro-electricity plant for the hours needed, the mine shut down the calciner.

Autumn's dampness arrived with the rolling morning fog or sometimes relentless curtains of fine mist that swept the town and mountain for much of the day yet left behind the street grime and mine rubble. Zillah was on her way to the grocer's the week before Easter, which came early in 1934, and as she turned into Main Street she saw two police vehicles outside the post office.

A small group of locals blocked the footpath and the sergeant was making useless attempts to shoo them away. "There'll be plenty to find out when the culprit gets to the courthouse," she heard him say.

She circled the group and recognised Kathleen's dad. "What's going on, Mr Kelly?" she asked. The 'closed' sign was on the door but it was wide open.

"Someone blew up the safe last night. If it hadn't been for the constable doing his rounds, they might have gotten away with it," Mel Kelly said, his voice low so he didn't attract the sergeant's attention.

Even standing there with the evidence all around, she found it hard to believe. In her quiet town, while she'd been sleeping, someone had broken a window at the rear of the grand old building and set gelignite. The thief had made off with cash boxes, stamps and postal notes worth nearly fifty quid.

"Turns out the baker, Arthur Spinks, got caught up in it," Kathleen's father half-whispered. Before

Zillah got the chance to find out more about what the baker had done, the sergeant began waving his arms and barking orders for them all to move on.

That evening, when she met Reg to go walking, he had the full story, told direct to him by Arthur Spinks' son, also called Reg and a football teammate. Constable Males had been on patrol about three o'clock in the morning when he'd seen a flash of light at the post office. He had found a side window broken and the blind flapping out the gap and, fearful there might be more than one thief, had run up the street to the bakehouse to get help from Arthur, doing his usual night shift. As they ran in different directions to cover the front and side entrances to the building, there had been three loud explosions.

"Oh Reg, it must have been awful. They wouldn't have known how many were inside or if they had guns."

He had been so busy telling the story it was only when he heard the fear in her voice that he registered the effect it was having on her.

"It's alright. It worked out in the end," he consoled her, waiting to see if she was calmer before he went on describing the incident. While the constable had been trying to get through a gate at the side entrance, a man had pushed past him and up the hill. The constable had chased after him and was only six or seven yards away when the man stopped and the copper saw a gun flashing at him in the torchlight. The constable had recognised the man. It was Percy Marsh from out at the Five Mile Camp and although Percy said "Stop or I'll shoot", the copper still went for him. The man fired but luckily, Reg told Zillah, he had missed.

"That's terrible. I don't think anything like this has happened before," Zillah said, her voice trailing off. Reg gave her wrist a squeeze.

"Arthur recognised him as well, so he's a goner. The sergeant and Males went out to the camp this afternoon and found the pistol and most of what was stolen, so they've got him."

They walked up towards the school for a bit then turned back to the centre of town and on towards her place, with him letting her set the pace. At the bottom of the street he checked to see if anyone was watching then kissed her on the cheek. She walked on alone, him keeping an eye on her progress from one streetlight to the next until she disappeared inside the yard.

Usually Zillah fell asleep the minute her head hit the pillow but tonight she lay there for a long time, staring out into the darkened room. It was ridiculous to feel so shaken by something that had not happened to her but it didn't seem to matter how much she told herself she was being childish, she still felt sickened. It was like it had happened here in her own home without her noticing, not a mile away.

She turned onto her side but barely had her hip touched the mattress when a tight wad of disquiet pressed against her ribs and she had to roll the other way, where it was no more comfortable. Back and forth she went, unpicking the minutes of one hour then two.

As she flung herself about in the bed, she remembered how the same sick feeling had clutched her belly during the big fires of '32. A heatwave in the New Year had ignited wildfires that raged for weeks. No-one knew how it had started in the bush down at the power station but the moment the slow burn had touched the sulphur-laden dead timber and soil towards the calciner, it had erupted, consuming the valley and racing towards the town with a dull, menacing whine unlike anything she had ever heard.

The updraft had powered solid pieces of burning timber up from the gorge and hurled them over businesses on the western valley rim. Thick smoke and burning sulphur had made it impossible to see the fire or to predict the direction it was moving. Within a day, the heat in the main street had been so terrible that, as she'd watched with Kathleen from the end of the railway bridge, she saw the post office catch fire. While men rushed to save it, flying embers set houses alight in the street behind.

The memory remained vivid—her standing above the railway station and knowing it was dangerous, that she should not be there at all. But as much as she struggled to breathe through the scarf tied over her face, she was bewitched by the frenzy set loose before her as firefighters ripped the iron off a house roof to get to its burning rafters and men ran shouting with buckets while the swollen hoses on the old Dodge fire truck fell flat as the water ran out.

The fumes pinched her nostrils and the air was so thick it seemed easier to eat it than draw it into her lungs but still she could not move, the action playing out like the film she had seen of Vesuvius spewing lava. Her town was unrecognisable, cowering beneath an explosive force that capable men could not control. It was Kathleen's common sense that broke through and she was fierce as she tugged on Zillah's wrist.

"We have to go! We have to go now!"

A surge of adrenaline shot through Zillah's chest and legs and the two women charged towards home on the eastern side of town, where houses were not at immediate risk.

Even at the top of Camp Road there was no escaping the effects of the fire. Day after day, her father and Eric returned blackened, their throats raw from the toxic air, worn out with the effort of standing shoulder to shoulder with other miners on the upper section of the steep valley, beating back the fire again and again from the stamper mills, desperate to hold onto their livelihood. They ate, fell into bed for a few fitful hours then returned to take another shift, while in the kitchen, Zillah and her mother kept up a steady supply of sandwiches, pasties and pies for their own men and for the emergency station the townswomen had set up at the council chambers.

Twice a day the junior constable, Michael Donovan, came to give the women an update, the youthfulness of his face stamped hard by strain. His house was also on the safer side of the valley but it was much closer to the fire than Zillah's and inside, where his wife tended their toddler son and baby girl, the air was as dead as Tutankhamun's tomb, the windows jammed shut and newspapers stuffed under the door to block the toxic fumes.

Zillah had thought the nightmare would never end but at the end of the month, heavy rain had quelled the fire. By some miracle, no buildings had been lost and few injuries sustained and it was a relief for everyone to return to their routine. Yet she hadn't settled so easily into the days and it had been a long time before she felt her world was restored, though it never quite felt that everything was back in order.

A FEW WEEKS LATER, Zillah was at a farewell sup-per for the Donovans in the hall at St Joseph's. Her mother had made sure Zillah and all her siblings were there to celebrate the constable's transfer to Strahan. The policeman's parents had farmed at Quamby, near Alice's family, so it was more personal than the fact that he was a Catholic. Besides, the poor man had been through a lot. He'd only been at Waratah a year when his wife had taken their first baby to meet his parents, retired and living in the coastal town of Devonport. During the visit, the constable's elderly father had died in the outhouse and when his mother discovered the body, she had collapsed with a heart attack and was gone soon after. Constable Donovan had arrived at the house to collect his wife and child and instead helped carry out his parents' bodies.

During the speeches, Zillah idly watched the constable nodding as he balanced his son on his hip but it was something in the man's face that soon caught her attention. She wondered if it was relief, if he was glad to be escaping the bush that pressed in all around to go to a town that, although still on the West Coast and isolated, at least opened out to the full breadth of a vast harbour.

4

"Stop that now and get outside," she shouted. At almost three years old Reg had never seen her face like that: swollen, her eyes without colour. Her hands trembled. She picked up a dishcloth as though she would tackle the table full of dirty dishes then dropped it before lifting the broom, which she set down without sweeping the floor.

In the corner in his crib, the baby Cliff began to cry with the urgency of an empty belly. She didn't seem to hear him and, instead, pointed at Reg. He dropped the tattered cricket ball, one thumb momentarily catching where the leather had ripped from the stitching, and ran out the back door. Twelve-year-old Doris was standing on tiptoe under the clothesline that was strung from a post near the side fence to the end of the house. When she saw him she put the handful of wooden pegs in her apron pocket and held out her arms. He rested his head on her bony hip while she patted his back.

At sixteen, Horrie was the oldest child still living at home but it was thirteen-year-old Allan who had the big axe, swinging it with all his might to cut the pieces of myrtle into kindling while Horrie stacked it.

"We could'a really done with Cec here now. Not much bloody good him and Tot in Melbourne, " Horrie said, spitting on the ground to cover the quivering in his throat. It had been hard enough before when he gave his mum ten shillings a fortnight for board and food but there was no way the pound notes in that envelope every second Thursday for driving the delivery stables' horses would be enough.

Cecil had married earlier that year and had done well for himself, by all accounts. Though he worked hard, it was no disadvantage to be wed at twenty-six to Margaret Kipling, who came with a handsome inheritance from her late father, a successful Bendigo businessman.

Tot, whose real name was Emma but they never called her that, had been gone even longer but the inheritance she'd married into was a scandal. Baptist Minister Reverend P.W. Cairns had said all the right things as they stood around in the 'good room' of the Sutton family's Burnie cottage, but "till death do us part" was not, it seems, in Francis Shepherdson's plan. Two months later he was gone, to look for work he said. He left behind his twenty-one-year-old bride, who would soon be grieving an infant born before its lungs were fit to do anything complicated like breathing.

The story had been all over the local and Melbourne papers the previous year, how Tot eventually had tracked Francis down at his parents' South Yarra home and he'd sent her packing because he couldn't support her. How later, the police had arrested him in New South Wales for bigamy and he had told the detective: "I know I've done wrong but I couldn't live with the first one".

In the end, the two things Tot had kept were his name and the belief that no man was worth it. Return to Burnie was impossible for her she'd said, and she stayed to make a new life in Carlton, far from any pitying gazes.

Inside the Wilmot Sreet house, Alice had no energy left for shouting. Her mind went to George and the way eight-year-old Cec and seven-year-old Tot had held on tightly to each of the widower's hands the afternoon she'd met them. They'd already been through their first Christmas without their mother and they had been wary. Alice had seen the obituary—their mother had been only thirty-three and in failing health for some time. She remembered looking at the two sad scraps in front of her and hoping that the boy would never read the newspaper article and discover that his mother's end started with his beginning; that the heart defect was most likely triggered by her first pregnancy.

"It's a big risk, taking on another woman's children," her own mother had warned, though she may as well have been talking to a stump for all the good it did.

Alice had seen her convict father claw his way up the ladder in Tasmania's narrow society to be acknowledged as "one of the island's most respected early colonists". This for a man banished from his home in Devon, England, and shipped out on the *Earl Grey* with nothing to his name but a ten-year sentence for stealing twenty-one pounds of cheese and three tattoos reminding him that he was once someone who mattered to others.

Her father had been a man of the earth in the old country, a ploughman and shepherd. In a new colony short on labour and skills, he'd been shrewd enough to know that making himself useful through hard work and a willingness to bend to the will of those with power would swing the odds in his favour. William Calway liked to brag about how, within five years, he had been granted a ticket-of-leave and begun working for wages again. A farmer at Kangaroo Bottom, down south, had seen the taut muscles and the determination in his eye and had given him a fresh start by taking him on as a roustabout. William had soon proven himself worthy as a trusted farmhand and, in time, had become a farmer himself. The orchard and seven-room brick cottage at New Town, where Alice and her siblings had grown up, were proof that a man could dare to make something of himself if he were fit and of a mind to.

Alice understood life as a series of shaky attempts to create certainty and she had decided that the lanky carpenter, with a steady business and a house he had built himself, was a solid chance. So, like her mother, she had married an older man and as their children arrived year after year, it had never occurred to her that he might not live well into his eighties. Her shoulders ached and her belly shook but after three days, there were no tears left to dampen the brittle tension snapping through her head.

The cancer had moved in quietly, content at first to claim a few small pockets of flesh, settling out of sight: white ants of malignancy working their way for months through the soft wood of membranes and moist tissue before George had felt anything at all. By then, it had grown strong and almost immediately, had begun gnawing insistently at hardy cells, including bone. Every time Alice turned away, she came back to find it had stolen a little more of the husband she knew, leaving another figure in his place. And all the while her belly had been swelling until, in the midst of her husband's slow dying, she had birthed a son.

The membrane of George's skin had shrunk as quickly as an animal pelt left in strong sunlight, stretching taut over bones where muscles, once hardened from lifting beams and punching nails, had dissolved into nothing. In the end, she had been afraid to leave him, even for a moment, in a hopeless attempt to guard what remained. How could this be? He was dead at fifty-six, leaving her with eight dependent children and the baby not yet three months old.

George's father had been a champion paling splitter

and in his prime had joined the gangs of men help-ing establish the Mount Bischoff mine, splitting and pit-sawing timber in atrocious conditions. Weakened by the rigours of work and climate, John Sutton had died in his mid-forties from measles. George had watched his six youngest siblings grow up fatherless. Now his own children would take their turn.

The Reaper's harvest seemed to favour her and the ones she loved. First her father, then her mother and—oh such pain—her beautiful twin sister Lucy, gone just like that in her twenties; all within six years of each other. George's death still did not seem real, even yesterday when his brother Edwin had placed his wide hand on her shoulder as he gently explained that he was off to take care of the formalities and register the death.

Near the woodshed, eleven-year-old Lucy, nine-year-old Owen and six-year-old Winnie shrieked and whooped as they chased the neighbour's scrawny cat. It ran through Reg's legs and leapt over the paling fence before he had a chance to see what was happening.

OVER THE NEXT THREE years, Reg grew into a for-getting of his father, who once had wasted away in the flesh but now disappeared as an idea, slipping away in random parts. First his frame vanished, then his voice, followed by the builder's hands and his eyes. Now, in July 1915, Reg no longer sensed the way his father's presence had once filled a room.

Cliff, who had rapidly progressed to walking then running, had no memories to forget. All the children, especially the older ones, were glad their mother no longer cried, though Horrie was still mad at Owen for taking off like that in the year after the funeral and stirring things up again. He and two friends had decided to walk fifteen miles west along the coast. They'd continued past Table Cape where it jutted out into the sea like an abandoned wheel of cheese, and found their way to the valley of Flowerdale next morning. By the time the coppers had found them that afternoon, Horrie had been ready to kill Owen for all the worry and his mother's sleepless night. "We just went for fun," was all the eight-year-old had said when they got him home.

Reg wasn't interested in walking a day and night for fun when he had a whole town to play in. He'd been the reason his mother had been fined two shillings and sixpence back in February for neglecting to send a child to school, her name listed for all to see in the local newspaper's Burnie Court report. His favourite place was the wharf he could see from his front gate. Days like today, when the *Excelsior* docked from Adelaide with a cargo of Lake MacDonnell salt, were the most exciting for the six-year-old. He had come to know most of the drivers who backed up their carts to load incoming cargo or deliver timber bound for the building boom in Melbourne.

Mostly the men would rouse him away, shouting: "No bloody place for a boy!" But once the unloading had begun and the crane would swing from the deck of the ship in a steady rhythm till the cargo was discharged, there would be no time for the men to do anything but keep pace with the work. Then Reg could get up close and find the draught horse he liked to pretend was his own.

Today he was in luck and soon found the big Clydesdale as it patiently waited for a load. This one was the steadiest, he thought, with dark green marbles for eyes, a thick brown mane and a wide back made for riding. Reg closed his eyes, feeling the boundary of his skin blur and dissolve. He could sense the horse's muscles and imagine the rocking rhythm of its big-stepping gait and, in that moment, he was no longer on the edge of the pier but stretched out along the sloping heat of its shoulders, his bones fitting smoothly into the solid curve, his arms hugging the horse's girth. There would be no Reg, no horse, just one rolling sway of power and purpose amid the hubbub and the smell of oiled leather.

The idea was delicious and he glanced towards a group of wharfies before dashing around to the other side of the dray in the hope of touching the creature. But he wasn't quick enough and one of the wharfies saw him and shook a fist in his direction.

Reg took off into the town centre where he found another horse, this one hitched to a pony trap outside the baker's. As he climbed up to the seat, the driver came out the door carrying a stack of trays with loaves. Reg ducked down and swung a leg over the other side onto the metal rim of the wheel, ready to slip out of sight.

The trays rattled as they hit the floor of the cart and the mare, out of habit, stepped forward and braced herself. The wheel rolled forward half a turn. Reg felt his left foot slip and he held on tight, fearful that he would fall on the ground and be seen, momentarily unaware that the driver catching him was the least of it, that his thigh was twisted in the spokes.

Around him everything seemed as it should, the smell of bread baking, the bell on the shop door, seagulls swooping over the breakwater cursing and squawking about each other's shortcomings. He was looking at a patch of dirt where a puddle was forming and it puzzled him because he knew it wasn't raining. It was then that the pain from his knee tore through his throat and in one breath that seemed it would never end, he screamed.

The driver took one panicked look and ran to the bridle, backing the horse one step then lifting Reg free of the cart's wheel and laying him on the ground. Another man ran to get medical help. When Reg looked down, he saw blood staining the top of his pants leg and his foot turned out in a peculiar angle.

A blanket appeared and covered him and the misshapen leg. He whimpered when they lifted him into the local doctor's Fiat, any attempt at holding back tears long gone. Every sway and bump churned his stomach and rattled his bowels. A voice droned on from the front seat and all it seemed to say was a name but each time he went out to meet it, to figure it out, there was only air where the shape of the letters had been.

He was struggling to stay awake when they arrived at the nearest hospital, the Devon at Latrobe, and was beyond any pain as arms lifted him onto a gurney and wheeled him inside. He heard a male voice he did not recognise, clear and matter of fact, ask: "Can you save the leg?" A woman with soft eyes and strong hands held a mask over his face and a sweet, heavy smell embraced him.

"A shocking accident," said the *Advocate* in its report the next day, 3 July 1915. "It is expected that he will recover." The scar on his left thigh and knee would still be visible almost two decades later when the doctor gave him his final examination.

When Reg came round after emergency surgery, he looked for a familiar face and, finding none, began crying and snotting even though he knew he should shut it. "What's happening? Where's Mum? I want my mum." Later, when they had transferred him to the children's ward, the sight of other small, anxious faces did nothing to make him feel better and he turned his body to the wall.

He was not sure if refusing to eat did the trick but the next afternoon, his mother arrived. He braced himself for a good telling off though it did not come. She took one look at his pale face and thought better of it, stroking his hair instead.

"You've been lucky, lad. The doctor says you'll be able to walk again just fine." She went to say something else but stopped herself, wiping her eyes with a rough sweep of the back of her hand.

Reg was in the Devon for two weeks before the surgeon decided he was well enough to be cared for at home. Despite the hospital discouraging family visits because they upset the children, Alice made the journey to the hospital for a second time before he was discharged.

The thigh had been badly torn and the knee had required surgery, but Reg had youth on his side and it was not long before the wounds were healing clean and firm around a long row of stitches. So, weeks later, he did not expect to see his mother start crying again. It was the year the war began to do things to his family and much of it was beyond the grasp of a boy.

Horrie was one of the first local lads to sign up, the enlistment officer carefully recording his details. Still a driver at a local stables, blue eyes, fair complexion, brown hair, five foot six, a Baptist: all true. Twenty years old on the enlistment record: not true. Horrie was only in his eighteenth year. He was assigned to the 26th Australian infantry and sent for training to Enoggera Barracks in Brisbane, where the battalion's heat-hardened Queensland men practiced drills alongside the Tasmanians. A man accustomed to his own particular sense of freedom, Horrie soon earned himself a three-day punishment for disorderly behaviour and using abusive language.

The Wilmot Street house was calmer and quieter without Horrie lurching in late, singing drunkenly or slamming doors and now there was some army money. Reg, glad to be home from hospital but with his leg still bandaged and useless, thought this was a good thing altogether and he directed his efforts to enjoying all the attention he was getting from his mother.

By the time Horrie landed at Gallipoli in September, Reg was able to put some weight on the leg and do simple exercises to build up the muscles. He didn't hear the cablegram delivery, caught up as he was in the struggle to get out of the backyard dunny, the wooden crutch jamming under the latch and pulling the door in hard on his good shin. "Bloody buggery thing," he said, but quietly so his mother wouldn't hear because a ragged leg was no protection from her wielding a sharp hand.

As he wrangled the crutches and the crook leg over the back step, he saw his mother sit down at the kitchen table, the slip of paper in her hand. The silence scared him.

"Horrie's in hospital in Alexandria," she said. He nodded as though he knew what that meant but all he had to go on was his own hospital experience, with custard every day and a selection of picture books from the Red Cross volunteers. They'd even given him a wooden truck, missing one wheel but he didn't mind because it was not something his older brothers had busted before it got to him.

His mother said no more, making a pot of tea to indicate a return to the flow of their day. Reg went along with it, slow to understand how much weight one piece of paper could carry. Over the next few days, though, he began to grasp its meaning in the urgent, whispered conversations with visitors, the tightness of her mouth, the way she clenched and unclenched her hands. Some new awfulness had arrived.

She sent an urgent letter to the army and, days later, an answer arrived in a few lines of tidy typing below an official crest. It said that Horrie was now in Ras-el-Tin convalescent home recovering from frost-bite. His mother slammed the letter onto the table in frustration at the lack of details.

"What if he's missing fingers or toes? How will he work? What the hell is really going on?"

The rapid-fire questions were hurting Reg's head and he was relieved when their neighbour turned up and she took charge of giving a response.

Soon after the New Year, Horrie made it back to Alexandria and then France to rejoin his unit just in time for the 26th's first major battle at Pozières at the end of July. A few weeks later there was a knock at the door and Alice's trembling hand took another cablegram.

Reg watched her through the doorway, scanning her face, muscles tensing, wondering if he should bolt or wait for her reaction. She said nothing for the longest while, looking in his direction with emptiness in her eyes, and it was only when she'd shuffled down the hall and swung the kettle onto the stove that she spoke.

"It's not good, boy, but at least he's alive." Her voice splintered.

This time Horrie had been wounded in action, a shot badly damaging his left elbow. Alice tried to ignore the rumours in town but when she heard that Horrie and some fellow soldiers were likely killed in action, she wrote another letter to the army. "I am very anxious," she told them.

Reg saw her fears played out every day and sometimes at night, when he heard her moving around the house instead of sleeping. It went on for a month, when she received a notice confirming that Horrie was alive and would return to Australia on the hospital ship *Karoola* in December.

As Christmas approached, Reg was less concerned about his brother returning than about what Santa might bring. What he really wanted was a train set but his mother thought that, what with the war and all, it might be a big ask for Santa. So Reg had decided to settle for a balsawood airplane model and some soldiers and a toy cannon.

A semblance of peace settled on the house when Horrie returned and 1917 rolled over, though, Reg thought later, he should have known it wouldn't last. In March, Allan enlisted. By now an apprentice baker, he helped fill the ranks of Tasmania's 40th battalion, joining the 8th Reinforcement. In June, he was on the *Hororata* on his way to England, where he sailed from Southampton to France, only to find his work with flour and yeast was no preparation for weeks bogged in the bloodiness of trench warfare in Flanders.

The months pressed on and, in December, the worry lines on Alice's face grew deeper when Allan was hospitalised and there was no information from the army to reassure her. The wait this time was brief, however, and in January 1918 she was notified her son had recovered and was on his way to the Somme Valley. In March, the battalion met the German Spring offensive at Morlancourt.

The news filtering through to Burnie was not

good, with the number of dead growing steadily and the daily casualty lists climbing even faster. As the tension in the house mounted, Reg no longer enjoyed playing with the lead soldiers. He found an old hanky and tied them up, shoving them under the mattress as far as he could so he would not be tempted to get them out.

His mother had to wait till early April before she got the official news. The battle of Morlancourt had ended early for Allan, who had been shot in the arm on the first day and was in Reading War Hospital in England. News was patchy and for Reg, leaning on the rail across the verandah, it seemed like there was always something upsetting the mood in the house, whether it was a neighbour's gossip, government announcements or the grey faces of local men returning with injuries.

Allan did not go back to the front. While his arm was healing he became seriously ill with appendicitis and was transferred to military hospital in Sutton Veny. Alice had heard the stories about soldiers dying from tuberculosis and the Spanish flu and her nights were fretful until the end of the year, when she was informed that Allan would be repatriated in early 1919. Later, all her worrying would be cause for guilt when she learned that 475 men in his battalion had died and her son had been just one of the more than 1700 wounded.

It had been a long haul, thought Reg, but at last he could get the toy soldiers back out and maybe his mother would stop complaining about him playing under her feet and making her trip when he couldn't even see what the heck was in her way.

5

January 1935 had given way to February and at the Athenaeum Hall, Zillah was one of the last to leave after helping to take down the badminton nets. She and her playing partner had lost yet another doubles match. "Ah well, at least we make the others look good," Zillah called back over her shoulder to Vera Paine, laughing as she went out into an unusually bright morning.

Reg was waiting in the shade near the toilets so she did not see him till he came up behind her. He looked terrible; the scorched folds of skin below his eyes were pink and raw. Her first thought was that something dreadful had happened to his mother.

"What is it, Reg. What's happened?" She wanted to hug him, hold him, but the council chambers and the police station were over the road and someone might see.

"My job's gone and I'll have to leave my room at the pub. Reardon's retiring and he told me last night he'll be gone in a fortnight and there'll be no work for me. Seems like the new licensee's got his own folks."

With John Reardon leaving, Reg had gone up the street to the Bischoff Hotel and asked after work but they had nothing. His mate, Cyril Alexander, was a barman there and he had talked to the pub's licensee, Ray Whyman. He could give him temporary work travelling around the district, collecting debts.

"Well that's good, isn't it?"

Zillah couldn't see why he was so downhearted, especially as it turned out that Cyril had offered to let him share his room at the Bischoff. Cyril and Reg's older brother, Allan, went back a long way, racing pigeons together for years, and though Reg thought Cyril had probably taken pity on him, it was still a generous offer.

"Yeah, I guess. It's probably the longest I've had the one job so I suppose I didn't see it coming."

She squeezed his elbow. "Reg, I'm really sorry."

He walked with her as far as the mine manager's big white house, its three-sided verandah with its wrought-iron lacework filling the corner where Smith Street met Corinna Road. They arranged to meet later and she headed towards home. Instead of going straight back to the hotel, he turned right and followed the road over the river then up the hill and past the school. He took every detour he could before slipping in through the hotel kitchen and up to his room.

He didn't know how long he'd been sitting on his bed but it must have been at least an hour because he could hear the chink-chink of dishes and plates being set for lunch. He would have to go downstairs soon to start his shift.

He stared at the blank wall opposite and as he did, his mind was no longer stalled but shifting and roaming without will, and the wall was the same but it was no longer white and it took a minute before he recognised the cold prison blue. He thought he'd put it behind him but he might as well have been sitting on that same unforgiving bunk, for all the prospects he had.

It had been 1931, in the hungry years. Jobs had been hard to come by but it wasn't as if that was anything new for a man like him who was only good for work as a labourer or painter. He didn't know the dapper Fred Lay all that well but they'd fallen in together on the road while looking for odd jobs and over a few drinks it had seemed like an obvious thing to do.

They'd pushed into the Circular Head district, in the far North West, where rolling dairy farms stretched inland from the sea and held the promise of a few weeks' work as farmhands. It turned out to be a dead end, both the road and the chance of earning a few bob running out where the surf thrashed in at Marrawah.

The pair backtracked, walking and camping out. Near Forest, they stole some potatoes from a farm shed and that night, over a fire and the smell of charred spuds, they cooked up a new plan. Next morning, at the fishing village of Stanley, they chose a property a mile or more from the police station with a house that had a garage some distance away. It didn't take long. They pulled out the wires to the battery and the starter motor and used their pocketknives to strip back a section of coating on each end before touching them to jumpstart the Dodge.

"Only six cylinders. Not going to win any races now there's a model out with eight," Fred said.

Reg was already at the wheel. "Get in, you can yap about that another time!"

At the main road they turned east, agreeing that Launceston might be their best chance for work. They stopped at a one-pump garage at Rocky Cape, filling up with the motor running and paying quickly before the owner had a chance to challenge them about why they hadn't killed the engine. They kept going through Burnie to Ulverstone, where Fred wanted to stop for tucker.

"No bloody way, Fred. I've played footy here and there's plenty who know my ugly mug. I'm not risking it."

As they tooled along the coast in the early afternoon, they were both hungry and their harmless banter about what they would do quickly escalated to a loud argument when Reg insisted they keep driving.

Fred reached for the door handle. "Stop and let me out then, Reg. I'm not having you telling me what to do."

Reg gave in and when they got to the next town, Westbury, Fred put in a rush order for fish and chips at a roadside café. Reg sat nearby in the car with the motor idling, out of sight behind a large hedgerow.

It was past four o'clock when they dumped the car near the railway workshops at Inveresk. The loud banging and hammering from the sheds drowned out the sound of the car being violently stalled in their rush to bail out. They were two very different men but as they hurried across the bridge towards the brewery and the workers' end of town, both were fighting the same corrosive urge to run for it and be damned. Instead, as they left the river behind, they deliberately loitered like mates who just happened to meet in the street.

They chatted casually, or so it would seem to those not close enough to catch their eyes flicking up and down the street, and then went in search of a bar. They hadn't placed the first order for a beer before the police were tipped off about which pub they'd headed to. It turned out the informant had fallen on hard times and he knew what the act of abandoning a car meant. Yes sir, it was a magic trick that turned a stolen car into a few bob from the coppers.

Though the courts were getting tough on theft, Reg was familiar with this belly crawl through the tight space of the law and did not expect to go to gaol. He steeled himself for a fine he couldn't pay and a lecture from Allan about upsetting their mum.

In early August he got sentenced to fourteen days

for illegal use of a car. He was halfway south to Hobart in the paddy wagon before his fate started to sink in.

Usually he had a cast-iron stomach and maybe it was because the road beyond Epping Forest was winding and there were no windows in the back of the van, in any case he ended up chundering ten minutes before they opened the rear door. He'd wiped the vomit off his shoes with a handkerchief and made a useless attempt to mop the rest off the floor before giving up and tossing the lumpy, sodden scrap under the bench. The curdled smell of his partly digested cheese sandwich followed him out into the Campbell Street Gaol reception yard.

"Dirty bastard," the older copper said, gripping him by the elbow with one hand and slamming another in his back to smack him towards the sergeant for sign-in.

They took photos to go on his records before he pulled on the prison grey. If he saw the pictures, he probably would have been the first to say that the bloke in the full-length version with the rumpled jacket and trousers looked a bit lost but the close-up showed a darn good-looking fellow. In the gaol, he kept to himself pretty much for the two weeks, did what he was told despite being tempted a few times to tell the warders what he thought, and was relieved when they marked him off and he was free to go.

He stood in the street with less than a pound in

his pocket and more than 200 miles to cover if he wanted to head back to Burnie. He looked towards the harbour and the tips of masts. Maybe he would go down there and sit for a while among the ships and the activity on the wharves to find some of the comfort and pleasure of his childhood. Perhaps even a passage to somewhere else.

The longer he waited the more it seemed like an effort and, after a few minutes, he came to the conclusion that he didn't really feel like going anywhere at all. Still, he thought, standing in the street would only draw attention to his worn jacket and the pants that were in need of an iron, so it was best to get moving.

At a nearby shop he bought a pack of 333 cigarettes and enjoyed the warmth radiating off the bricks while he leaned against the side wall to have a smoke. He walked for a while and when he fluked on finding New Town Road and the route to the north, he consoled himself by pretending his luck had changed. "See, mate," he told himself, "it's not so bad after all, and you're still young and fit".

The road took him out to Granton and by early afternoon he'd convinced a truckie at the roadhouse to give him a lift. "No suitcase, fella?" the truckie asked, laughing at his own joke as Reg swung himself up onto the seat.

Reg knew the bugger was only having some fun to

make the time pass when he could see he was hardly a man on holiday, but as the truck strained up the hills he had not expected the driver to ask so many questions. He stuck it out for what seemed like the best part of an hour but he was desperate to be on his own. He got the fellow to let him out at Kempton.

The town was a single strip of buildings huddled on either side of the road, dominated by former coaching inns in need of care and occasional double-storey mansions built for gentleman graziers with profits from merino sheep. Joining the dots were leaning cottages, a few shops and a church here and there. Any minute he expected the old tinker who hung around these parts, Mrs One-eyed Brown, to appear in her creaking cart and try to sell him a few homemade pegs.

He walked past the rows of windows, picking up a bit of speed near the police station. He pulled up the collar of his jacket in a vain attempt to hold back a cutting southerly straight from Antarctica and kept going till he found the sportsground. On the lee side of the grandstand, he lit a smoke and tried to look casual, like a man who was on the way to somewhere, in case anyone had spotted him. After he stubbed the cigarette out with his boot, he checked carefully in all directions then slipped around the corner. The men's toilets had their back to the road and although they were locked, an alcove at the door provided shelter.

As daylight retreated and took with it the view of the oval, he bunkered down in the corner, ignoring thoughts of roast beef or a few fried eggs.

Sleep was a long way off. He found himself searching his mind like it was one of the many-roomed mansions down the road and in the attic he might find something he dared hope for: one bright, shiny thing worth the striving. Perhaps a job that would last for more than a few months? A girl who wouldn't mind if he put an arm around her and pulled her in close so he could feel her, warm and full of life? His own place, where he could shut the door and forget about all that was impossible, all that the world seemed to demand of him?

He slapped his arms in a vain attempt to generate some heat. There was no mansion he thought, annoyed at his own imagining, not even a one-room shack with a lean-to out the back. Every possibility he landed on turned to ash blown to nothing by the wind.

"Snap out of it," he murmured, but it didn't stop the useless words from circling, rattling the can of his empty life. "Dust to dust," they said, "world without end, you're a loser-loser-loser, never amounting to anything." Try as he might to switch them off, the voices in his head kept talking a torrent of shit. He was relieved at last when the load of exhaustion took him down into oblivion.

From Kempton, he took his time, sleeping rough

and relying on his wits as he made his way up to the coast. He walked some days and on others hitched a lift for as long as he could tolerate the drivers.

It was almost midnight when he was dropped off near the Mersey River at Devonport. It was high tide and the river was in full flow, restless against the wharf while the town slept. For years, vessels had steamed in from Melbourne and Sydney with a secret cargo of shipworms burrowed deep in their timber hulls. The river had siphoned out the tiny molluscs and dumped them at the hardwood piles of Victoria Bridge, where they had tunnelled into the bridge's wooden supports and structure, leaving thousands of drill holes on the surface. The decking echoed as Reg crossed wide sections of the bridge, rattling where the timber had been patched.

His left foot dragged when he was tired, like it had done since the accident as a kid, so it took a while before he reached the town centre. He was stewing on whether it was such a good idea to continue on to the bluff in search of a sheltered place to get his head down. Though the beach curved inside the hook of the headland it was exposed to a raw wind that cut the tops off waves in Bass Strait like a butcher slicing meat from bone, one powerful sweep after another.

Through the big window of a grocer's shop in the main street, Reg could see bins of apples, tins of soup and fish, and shiny brown bars of Pears soap. The sight of the food set off a wave of hunger but even stronger was the desire to get his hands on a bar of the soap and get himself clean. For the first time since he left the gaol, he could not stand the acid stench of the clothes he had slept in or the prickly skin that itched and chafed in moist creases behind his knees, in his groin and between his toes.

Breaking in wasn't too hard. Around the back in the shadows, he found an old timber door with a large brass lock and rusting screws. He slammed a foot against the door. It took three goes before the screws tore away from the timber and then he was in, stuffing a hessian bag from behind the counter with food, matches, tobacco, candles, washing powder— whatever he could carry. Ten minutes later, away from the town and hidden by a grove of casuarinas, he dropped his clothes on the stones by the river and soaped himself all over, rinsing off quickly with handfuls of water so cold it bit to the bone. Despite shivering it felt good, even after he'd buttoned up his stale shirt and pulled on the shapeless pants.

A couple of days later, he made it to the outskirts of Burnie but there was no way he was ready to show up at his mother's house. He didn't need a mirror to know he was barely recognisable and it seemed like he had nothing to offer in walking through her door. He joined a handful of itinerants and set up camp near them in one of the stock pens at the Wivenhoe

Showgrounds, ignoring the tang of dried sheep droppings and cow dung. He was still camping there when the trooper turned up and inspected what was left in the hessian bag. What a sorry damn business, with the end already sorted before he was carted off to the station.

Things moved fast and he did his best at mounting a defence but it was a waste of time, especially once the detective told the bench he had a bad record. The hearing was over in fifteen minutes and he left the court under police escort, though this time it would be a three-month stretch.

Outside the court he felt edgy; his instinct was to make a run for it and hang the consequences, especially when the copper was only half his muscle and bulk. But he'd already been stupid once, keeping the stolen goods instead of ditching what was left over, and there was no denying that he had a bloody knack for taking bad times and making them worse.

In his narrow cell in Hobart, the despair oozed cold from the walls, carrying the shadowy presence of the convicts who'd built them brick by brick, and after a few weeks it began to soak into his spine. He was caged in for long hours with no natural light in a cell so small that when he bent over to pull up the blankets for inspection, he had to be careful he didn't bump his bum on the wall opposite and knock himself over.

They were locked up for the duration of every

weekend and he never thought he would welcome the chance to line up on a bench with other men the way he looked forward to the diversion of a Sunday visit to the prison chapel. By the end of the first month, he knew every tiny flaw in the grout near his bed and his ears were so finely tuned he could tell what was happening in each cell in the northern block by the sounds of the others and more kinds of silence than he had ever known.

It got to him after a while, making it harder to stick by the rules than before. Reg felt the sharp teeth of desire growing in his gut. He'd heard the stories about blokes going mad in the dark in the solitary cells in the southern end and was careful not to do anything that might land him in there, but the beast in his belly was rising. He got an extra seven days for stealing from one of the screws, swiping a near-empty pack of cigarettes that had fallen out of the warder's shirt pocket as he was escorting them to the exercise yard.

The days he was boxed up in the tiny blue cell were unbearable and there were times when he wondered if the scaffold facing the Brisbane Street wall of the gaol might be a better option. But the last man had dropped through the trapdoor nearly a decade earlier after murdering three men, including his cousin and a trooper, so it wasn't as if the hangman got much practice.

He hated everything about doing time. The pigswill

slapped onto a tin plate at midday parade, the stink of the slop bucket in his cell, the eyes always watching, the sense of someone at his back with a sharpened screwdriver up his sleeve. For weeks, a fellow in the damp cell next door—only a few years older than him and inside for burning down the house of his wife's fancy man—had wheezed his way through a bout of pneumonia. He'd been carried out in a box.

His cell had two doors, an inner wooden door with a bulging Jackson padlock and an outer door with an iron grille and neat mortice lock. He loathed the first half-hour of the day from 6 am, when the screws unlocked the inner door and the men further up the corridor on the upper level, where he was located, mooched past to go for a wash. Every head faced to the front but at each grille, the men rolled their eyes to the right and in one quick scan sized up a cell and the person in it. Reg had learned this skill, too, the first time. Hunter or hunted, inmates only got two choices here. He liked it better when the wooden door slammed shut and he no longer had to fill up his skin so he didn't look like quarry.

The gaolers had their hierarchy—the governor at the top, followed by his weaseling clerk, who although he was a prisoner was favoured by the big man and had to be kept onside. Then came the deputy governor and the three overseers, in charge of the gaol's bootmakers' shop, bakehouse and the big workshop for carpentry, blacksmithing and tin-smithing. The warders were next, the older fellows trading sly knowledge of shortcuts and intimidation methods, while the younger ones were sent to search cells for smuggled goods and retrieve parcels pushed under the Brisbane Street gate—brown paper hiding hacksaw blades, cheese, clean underpants, anything a man would be willing to trade for. On the lowest rung were the scum, prisoners who were wardsmen but came in handy because they did the tedious and grubby work of distributing brooms for the men to sweep their cells, taking breakfasts to the cells at 7 am and the dinners in the evening, and hauling wood and coal for the bakehouse and governor's quarters.

The prisoners' pecking order was far simpler. At the top were a handful of men, notably Henry "Knocker" Price, who was getting a longer stretch after a break-out and recapture soon after he was banged up five years earlier. Ropey, and with quick reflexes, Knocker was fair in that he lashed out indiscriminately and he had a strong philosophy on humanity, which he understood deeply as the equivalent of a fist in the face. His name came from his favourite saying: "For two pins, I'd knock your head off."

Next came the men who walked tall and proved themselves useful, filching a few favours or trading dice for two-up, a few cigarettes or a saucy postcard. Reg aimed himself there, though he avoided the braggards and the cocky ones. Then came the cowed, the ones who had given up, and below them were the mental defectives who were kept apart for exercise in Yard No.1. Last of all were the wardsmen and the view of them was the one thing the prison population shared with the gaolers.

Towards the middle of the second month, early on a Sunday morning, Reg had been let out of his cell to wash. As he moved towards the stairs that led down to his yard and washroom, warder Walker was approaching, boots drumming on the tongue-and groove-verandah. All the cells were open to let the second round of prisoners go down for a sluice and it was odd to see a warder coming back this way.

Reg automatically flicked eyes right as he passed Knocker Price's cell. Partly hidden behind the wooden door, with his pants around his knees, was Jimmy Hogan, one of the mental defectives. Reg knew it was him because in the furtive glance he saw the boots were tied with elastic and not laces. On his knees nearby was Knocker, with his flies undone.

Reg's spine was steel as he kept advancing down the verandah. He'd taken three paces past the cell when the warder got to the open door and looked in. Jimmy let out a mighty roar and burst out, shoving Walker backwards before the warder forced Jimmy back into the cell. Another warder was running from below, taking the stairs two at a time. Reg heard the thud of knuckles on soft flesh and knew, warder or no warder, that it was Knocker delivering the punch. It took the two screws, each holding an arm behind Knocker's back, to wrestle him down the stairs. A third warder came for Jimmy and shepherded him away, barking at the prisoners who'd gathered to get back to their cells.

Reg dipped his head back towards the action then kept moving. He'd no desire to be a witness to anything or to make himself a target.

At 9.20 am they were all let out again to make their way to each of the seven yards for church muster. The deputy-governor arrived with the muster books and began calling out the names of those attending the service; today it was for the men who had declared Church of England as their religion. Reg listened for his name and looked around for Knocker but there was no sign of him as the gaoler in charge unlocked the door underneath the balcony and led them into Yard 7, the closest to the church. From there another door was unlocked and they were taken into the chapel, where Reg took his seat on a bench in the upper tiers, separated from local residents who came in off the street to sit in boxes at the front.

"He'll get off, he always does," Keith Wrathall said, without moving his lips, after he'd singled out Reg to sit beside him. "Walker's keys went missing in the fight and you can bet Knocker's involved in that."

Reg stared at the pulpit, his line of sight broken only by the bobbing head of Jimmy Hogan on a lower bench. He shifted his weight forward, his hands gripping his thighs and his shoulders pushed back to stretch without drawing attention to himself. But it didn't help. The dread was still balled up tight in his belly.

Reg worked much of each weekday in the tinsmithy alongside Knocker, making registration plates for cars, as well as baking trays, billies and anything else the gaol could sell. Even to Reg, it seemed an odd choice to have a former escapee in a workshop where he had access to files, tongs and tinsnips.

Reg had met Knocker's type on the outside. Men who took the corner spot in a bar and held court with tall stories pumped even bigger by the beer and the hunger for a moment in the sun. They locked eyes on you and made a claim, whether you wanted it or not, the way that parched ground obliterated the first raindrops that fell when a drought broke. A man like Knocker didn't care about free will, only about what he could get and how soon.

After church, they were locked back in their cells so Reg didn't find out what happened to Knocker until he returned to the tinsmithy next day.

"Didn't expect to see you here," Reg said, under his breath.

"They needed to get the keys back more than they needed to do me for assault," Knocker said, tapping off an excess blob of solder so he couldn't be heard talking.

Knocker had done the warders a deal. He would get the missing keys back if they pretended nothing had happened. He knew he had them in the place that hurt because only the week before the warders had had their pay docked after one of them had hung a set of keys on a hook in the bakehouse and only turned his back for a minute before the keys were gone. They'd searched all the cells and the yards for four days before they found what they were looking for, under a flagstone in a small shed below the stairway to Yard 3.

While Reg had been in the chapel the day before, Knocker had retrieved the keys from the wood yard. The warders had asked for no explanation and Knocker had given none.

"You only need the one key to open a hundred doors, you know," Knocker said. Reg raised his eyebrows by way of a nod.

"I had a good gander at the keys."

Reg kept filing off the rough edges of the number-plate in his hand, turning one shoulder towards the bench where two men were melting lines of solder to attach handles to tin mugs, giving a sign that he did not want to hear any more. But Knocker was not one for subtleties and pressed on.

"You've only got a month and a bit to go, haven't

you?" he asked in the way of a man who already has the answer. Reg raised an index finger to confirm it.

"You're a smart fella. I could make it a bit easier for you, get you a few favours."

Down the other end of the workshop, near the blacksmith's bellows, a prisoner started banging a curve into a fiery bar of iron. There it was, Reg thought. No scales of justice but a balancing act just the same: predator or prey.

"What's in it for you?"

"Just a small ask, that's all. You in?"

"Depends. As much as the food's fantastic and the view's amazing, I don't want to stay any longer than I have to at Her Majesty's Pleasure."

Knocker kept his head down but Reg saw him grin. The workshop hubbub momentarily subsided and Reg took the numberplate to the finished pile and picked up the next one, carrying it back to his bench while Knocker was called away to take his turn at the tin press.

When Reg collected his midday meal, the shiny gristle wobbled in a watery mess and he abandoned his usual habit of three guesses at what animal it once had been. He picked at the food, eating a little only because the next serving, after lock-up, would be no better.

Back in the tinsmithy, Knocker sidled up as they returned to the workbench.

"What have you got in mind?" Reg wanted it out in the open.

"Just one thing. And if you say anything to anyone, you'll be mincemeat and there's others who'll help make sure of it."

"Understood."

"All you have to do is swipe me a decent piece of lead."

"You've got as much chance to do it as me, Knocker."

"Yair, but they keep more of an eye on me than you."

At that moment, they were interrupted by the overseer roaring at them from behind about more action and less lollygagging, then hooting with laughter at his own clever joke at Knocker's expense about getting caught fooling around the day before.

The afternoon dragged on. Reg was itching to finish this with Knocker so he could have a night behind the big wooden door to think things through. Just before half past four, they lined up for Harrison to count the tools back in. Knocker was behind Reg.

"So?"

There were a million things Reg wanted to say, about not getting dragged into the sewer with the rats, just needing to keep his head down and get out of here; about wanting a life and not some knock-down round in a ring with Knocker or a bigger boot up the bum from the law.

But all he said, under his breath, was: "Yair. Don't tell me any more."

"Not intendin' to," muttered Knocker, shuffling forward in the queue.

Reg didn't want to arouse suspicions so next day he avoided Knocker in the workshop and Knocker, for his part, did the dance of agreement as they moved about their tasks.

It was another two days before Reg had reason to be near the shelves with the supplies. He scanned the small collection of lead pieces, which were at eye level, then bent down to flick a couple of imaginary metal filings off his sock. Knocker didn't need to tell him: he knew any piece he snatched had to be at least the length of a key. He swallowed hard. Parallel lives stretched before him: one that went on much as before, the other tipping slowly for the slide down a mountainside where either a sheltering shack waited below or a pack of roving wolves.

As he straightened up, all thought stopped. He leaned a little towards the shelf and swept the closest suitable lump of lead off the edge and down onto the thick leather glove he wore on his left hand to protect it from the sharp edges of the rego plates. He held the glove firmly against his hip and moved back to the bench. The overseer was nearby, rounding on a young bloke who'd cut a piece of flashing too short for a repair under way on the roof of the bootmakers' shop.

With both hands under the bench, Reg transferred the lead to the inside of his glove and looked around for Knocker.

"What do you think you're up to?" Reg jumped. Harrison was at his shoulder, leaning in.

"Get your hands on the bench!"

Reg placed the gloved hand and his right hand on the benchtop in front of the overseer, pressing firmly so his bare hand didn't betray the shuddering rise and fall of his ribcage.

The prisoners continued to measure and saw timber, stretch tin plate and wield a hammer at the anvil but every pair of ears was there at the bench with Reg.

"Show me your hands."

Reg turned both hands over, palms facing up and fingers lightly curled, thumbs turned in, the glove still on. He pressed his tongue against the roof of his mouth, tasting metal as if the lump of lead was hidden there yet he could feel it lodged against the hollow at the base of his thumb.

Harrison clicked his teeth and crossed his arms. Reg waited, suspended in the moment like whitecaps riding the northerlies at West Beach, not knowing if the surf would carry them to shore or dump them when the wave pitched under.

The overseer leaned forward and pushed his wide face in front of Reg's.

"Orright. So now we know you've got a pair of

hands, use the bloody things!" And with that, he was gone to the men toiling on a new mouse-proof cupboard for the gaol kitchen.

The lead dug into the web of Reg's hand as he worked on one numberplate after another on the long downhill run to lock-up time. He kept looking for Knocker so he could transfer it before it burned through the glove but Knocker stayed out of his way. Just as Reg thought he would have to slip it out and leave it on the floor, Keith appeared beside him and pointed to his boot in a gesture that was commanding and impossible in equal measure.

Harrison made the call for tool line-up and Reg reached over with his right hand as though he would remove the glove but instead, slipped two fingers inside and hooked out the lead, holding it inside the leather opening, uncertain about what to do next. In a flash, Keith had it and was gone.

Back in his cell, Reg knew what would come next. He knew because a footy mate had a father who was a locksmith and he'd once explained how a thief could make a duplicate key on the sly. First, you shaped up a dud key from a lump of lead, making it look roughly like the original, based on a surreptitious look at the size and shape. Then you pushed the lead key into the lock and turned it back and forth a few times so the inside workings of the lock made marks in the softer lead, showing the pattern for the bit. After that, anyone with a bit of nous could file an iron key from the lead pattern. If the screws ever discovered he'd set the whole thing in motion, he might not get home for a long time.

Day after day, his nerves a mess of fencing wire pulled against a strainer post, he worked at staying out of Knocker's way. The feeling seemed to be mutual and after a few weeks, the tension eased and Reg could breathe without thinking there might be a price to pay for taking his share of air.

He was less than a fortnight from freedom when warder Anderson unlocked both cell doors. Word had it that Anderson had worked in England's infamous Bristol Gaol, where warders had the pleasure of birching prisoners into obedience. His eyes certainly carried the look of a man itching to apply a set of rods to bare shoulders.

Anderson began searching the cell. Reg knew something was up because cell searches normally meant two warders working their way through thirty at a time, but his was the only one unlocked. Anderson went straight to the mattress and lifted it, pulling out a pack of playing cards from the gap in the bunk corner where it was wedged. It was a small but satisfying triumph for the warder.

"Your kind, you never learn," he snarled, and turned as though to leave. But at the door he lurched back purposefully, powering his full body weight up from his feet to whack Reg on the side of the head with the hand carrying the cards. The blow knocked Reg's head against the wall but he managed to stay on his feet.

He got an extra five days for the cards, which had been passed on by a crony of Knocker's as one of the promised favours. The episode was a friendly warning to keep his mouth shut; Knocker's way of reminding him that his knuckles had a long reach.

Every day afterwards was a slow footslog, from the unlocking of his cell in the mornings till he was safe behind the thick wooden door that night. It was not so much that he believed Knocker would try to put the wind up him again—after all, he wanted to ensure he stayed quiet, not push him over the brink to a confession and making a deal with the screws—but he was burdened by the possibility that Knocker would press him into further service.

When they let him go, he was glad to be shot of the place. He didn't say a word to a soul about taking the piece of lead, not even a few weeks later when he was back on the coast and the papers were full of the details of the manhunt after Knocker, Keith and Jimmy had broken out.

After his release, he turned away from making a career of petty thievery, unlike Fred, who kept trying to take what he needed instead of earning it and, as a consequence, did hard labour more than once.

A menace to society was how one magistrate had described Fred and that was not a tag Reg wanted stuck to him. Yet sitting here on the bed in the pub he still felt marked, in the ugly way that ink bled around the edges of a badly drawn tattoo.

A rapping started up at the door, startling Reg. "Shake a leg, you're needed in the bar," Reardon bellowed.

Reg took off his jacket and slung it over the chair then went onto the landing, past the housemaid kneeling to wax a deep scratch on the dark mahogany banister. She took one look at his face and stood up, trying to catch his eye.

"Cheer up, you can be sure whatever it is has already happened."

He ignored her brassy good cheer and ran down the stairs, rolling up his shirtsleeves as he went.

6

Once a month the priest from Burnie drove in and so, on Sunday afternoon, Zillah and her younger brothers, little Jean and their mother put on their best hats and coats and left for mass. As they straggled up Main Street and approached the Waratah Hotel and its impressive double verandah, Reg came out the side door and hurried down the footpath. He was only a few yards away when he raised his head and saw her, giving a quick smile.

Zillah, walking beside her mother with the others scuffing and trailing behind, watched as Reg tipped his hat in Alice's direction, stepped to the same side as Zillah and waited for her. Stiff and red-cheeked, Zillah walked right past him without even a nod and the family continued on to the church, where they sat in the pew next to Alice's sister and the rest of the Randall family.

Reg remained motionless, looking back, the shadow of his hat low on his face.

There was no sign of him when the Housego family came back down the hill an hour or so later. The silence of Sunday, the one day of the week that the twenty batteries at the stamper mill lay quiet, buzzed in Zillah's ears like a persistent march fly. Phil, following close behind, accidentally clipped her heel with the toe of his boot. "Watch your step," she hissed, shoving her surprised brother away.

Tea on Sundays was always a light meal. As soon as she had changed from church, Zillah started preparing the Welsh rarebit without waiting to be asked. She sawed off thick slices of soft white bread and toasted them on a fork in front of the firebox, then pulled the saucer with a lump of cheddar cheese from the meat safe and banged the cheese onto the table along with a bottle of Worcestershire sauce. As she reached into the cupboard for the mustard, her mother paused as she bent in front of the fire, the poker in midair.

"You're in a mood, my girl," she said.

Zillah understood the observation for what it was: an instruction to stop irritating her mother. Her father had returned to his camp after the earlier roast beef and Isobel and Eric were out, so it was a quieter meal when the family pulled up their chairs to the table. She watched the toast with its cheesy sauce disappearing fast from the plates, with not a mention of the effort it had taken to prepare it. Watching her mother wash up and Jean dry the dishes, it was the image of tomorrow's tea and all the meals to come that was stuck on the inside of her eyeballs.

Agatha Christie was one of her favourite authors but as she attempted to read the last chapter of *The Murder at the Vicarage*, all she could see was an endless row of patterned plates. She gave up on the book and went to bed early.

Monday evening when Kathleen came for tea and to stay the night, Zillah slipped out about eight o'clock and met Reg near the railway station. They walked up the hill towards the school while she chatted about her day, desperately wanting to talk about what had happened on the way to church and how she had ached afterwards, but unsure how to start.

"Do you like me, Zillah?"

She stopped and turned to face him, wanting to give an answer but not finding any reply that could match the weight she sensed in the question.

"Really, I'd like to know." His voice was urgent.

"Of course I like you, Reg." They'd passed the only streetlight on the hill so it was hard to read his face.

"It's just that, you've never asked me home or even spoken to me in front of your brothers or Isobel."

Zillah went to make a joke about how ugly the rest of them were and how she didn't want to frighten Reg but then thought better of it. He was jumpy and she could tell from his voice he was in no mood for teasing.

"Reg, you don't understand. It's not that simple for me."

"Well, I'd like for you to meet my mother and the others. They might not be Micks but they do a good day's work and keep food on the table," he said.

"I'd really like to meet your family," Zillah said, "but I need more time for everyone at home to get used to the idea of us."

"How can they get used to anything if they never meet me?"

This was getting difficult, Zillah thought. She couldn't go upsetting her mother and she couldn't ignore Reg's rising tone or the hurt in his voice. If the tense band around her chest got any tighter, she would crack a rib. She just wanted to run home to Kathleen and talk about what they'd do tomorrow and who had the coldest feet as they topped and tailed in the single bed.

"Zillah, we've been seeing each other for a while now and we get on really well. I know I'm not much of a catch right now, working in a pub and all, but what matters is that I want to marry you and I'll do my best to look after you always."

He was almost pleading and on impulse she took his hand, holding it tight, aware that he seemed smaller here away from the light. Her voice came out soft but a little shaky with the effort of forcing herself to tell him something he would not want to hear.

"I like you well enough to marry, too, Reg, but I can't see how it could happen. You're a good man and it's got nothing to do with who you are or the money you make, you know that." She didn't want to go any further.

"Then marry me! Why not start a life together?" He was goading her now, pushing her to spill out the answer where it could get air and a proper examination. She accepted the challenge.

"Mum would never agree to me being wed to someone who's not Catholic and I couldn't go against her wishes. I'd want to marry with her blessing."

Just the thought of her mother's reaction made Zillah flinch. It was a fact that the whole Hartnett bunch was praised for their devout contribution to Catholic churches from here to Launceston. Despite her family's modest circumstances and need of greater income, Alice was proud in the knowledge that her brother, Dennis, a schoolteacher and bachelor still living in the area where they had grown up, had prepared a will that would leave his estate for the purposes of the Catholic Church and for regular mass for repose of the souls of their parents.

Zillah was dangling from a complex web and she didn't want to think about all that was trapped with her in the sticky threads. A mixed marriage meant there could be no ceremony at the front of a Catholic church. At best, you got a quick version at the side altar with the priest's lips pursed and the guests, if they dared attend, keeping their eyes down. Or you could leave the Catholic way for another house of God but your family would refuse to attend and any future children would be damned.

It went in both directions and plenty of Protestant fathers had disinherited daughters and sons for the grubbiness of marrying Catholics. If that wasn't difficult enough, you could be creating a family with a fault line through the middle, like her friend Mary and her dad siding with the Catholic ways while the younger brother went to St James's with his mother—and who knew how that might end.

The dividing lines between Irish Catholics and the world were clear and so were the rules about crossing them, but that was not what most troubled Zillah. As much as she wanted to be with Reg and as much as she might even take on her older brothers, she could not risk her mother's ire.

"Mum's a strong-minded person." Zillah was still holding his hand and looked up at him for a sign of compassion.

"But she hasn't had a chance to get used to the idea of us being together. She might see it differently if she gets to know me, sees how I care about you," he said, pinpricks of irritation breaking through his voice.

"I don't think she'd take a set against you personally, Reg. It's just that she wants all of us kids to marry within the church. She won't back down." Zillah was getting flustered and hadn't meant to sound so definite.

"Then what's the use, Zillah?" His reply cracked like a whip, loud in the thin air. He shook her hand free and marched off.

He'd never shouted at her before and her body froze, as though she'd been slapped. Her hands went to her chest and it was a long moment before she felt her lungs swell to take in a breath. As they did, her body impelled her forward and she found herself running after him and off the edge of any territory she knew, fearful and uncertain.

She caught up with him near the school gate. His stride slowed and she was alongside him. "Please Reg, please give me some time, I just need some time. I want to make you happy, I want us to be together."

The panic in her voice sounded foreign to her ears and she wanted it to stop but it kept coming, on and on, and it was out of control like the fire that had roared up the valley years before. Even as she heard it there was no sense it was her own.

A light drizzle had begun and she felt the moisture pooling on her face and in her hair and when she stopped talking and touched his sleeve, it was damp. He was leaving her to fill the space; it was like he had already gone. She cast around for anything she knew about what to do next but it was instinct coming to meet her and an animal body that stood alongside him. She looked across the valley. The starry night had fallen down onto the town and its lights were shimmering in the streets and windows, leaving the sky alone in cloud.

It took a while for her to calm Reg, using the same soothing tones that settled Jean after a bad dream, but she had no idea what she said because it seemed another woman stood in the rain and talked that man back to ground. He was speaking to her again by the time they parted near the post office but saying only the odd few words to be civil and, she noticed, he didn't apologise when he said he wouldn't walk her home.

Striding down the main street after dark on her own felt strange when she had always been with girlfriends, family or Reg. The shops loomed up one by one as she approached, their doors locked and the blinds pulled down. Towards home, at the mine manager's house, a soft wash of light came through curtains on the ballroom windows, though it had been years since the last party had been held there. In Camp Road, the streetlights were fussing about the moisture, fizzing loudly as she passed below them. She had walked by on many damp evenings before but she noticed it tonight for the first time. She was wrung out when she opened her bedroom door and pleased to find Kathleen asleep.

Next morning, before Kathleen left to go home, Zillah found herself sharing some of the previous night's events but only the proposal and her dismissal of it, playing it down. She made no mention of any anger or angst so her friend wouldn't have cause to say anything to family here or at her own place.

Kathleen was not so easily deterred. "Would you marry him if your mother approved?"

"I think I would but it's hard to know because

Mum's not going to agree so there's no point you asking that."

"Well why keep seeing him, Zillah?" This was making no sense to Kathleen, who had only once had a crush on a boy, in Grade 5, but had abandoned it when he propelled a giant spitball into her hair from the back row.

"We get on and he's a good friend, so why should I stop seeing him? It's not all about a wedding ring, you know." The logic sounded rickety, even to Zillah, but it put a halt to her friend's questions.

Her mother took the motor car service to Burnie the next day, leaving her to take care of chores until she returned with the shopping late that evening. Zillah was glad to have a full day of cutting wood, stoking the stove, cooking, cleaning and mending. As much as she was desperate to see Reg and to know if he still cared, she was jittery and the feelings put her in mind of the day she'd gone with her schoolfriends to the Fill-em Dam, which was out of town and away from adult eyes.

She and a group of girls had finished swimming in the shallow edge of the water and were sunning themselves, legs dangling over the warm stones of the wall at the deep end of the dam while the older boys dive-bombed each other. She'd been checking a sunburn blister on her friend's neck when two of the boys had sneaked up behind and pushed her in.

After flapping and squealing in the cold water while the girls squawked louder than hens with a quoll in the chookhouse, she'd been fished out by one of the boys. She still had enough energy left to give him a good thumping before she stormed home but she had never gone near the wall again.

The following morning she was scraping moss off the timber around the small panes of glass that made up the one window in the bathroom. She was going carefully with the knife so she didn't take too much paint with it and cause a set-to with her mum, when she heard knocking at the front door and her mother's heavy tread go up the passageway.

Rarely did anyone knock at the front door and if they did, it was usually Frankie Kovac on his round from Burnie with his van, selling whatever bargains he had bought in bulk. One month it might be tennis racquets, the next tea towels but always with a story to share, which meant her mother might be at the door for some time. So it was a shock when she went into the kitchen ten minutes later to find Reg at the table and her mother sitting opposite, their voices low.

"Reg tells me he wants to take you to Burnie to see his mother. It's not something I can agree to."

Zillah was dumbstruck and looked at Reg for a clue, any sign to indicate what on earth was going on.

"Yes, Mum misses the girls. She doesn't get a lot of visitors these days and she'd enjoy your cheerful ways and chat, I reckon. I've got to go on Thursday for a night and I thought it might work out." Reg spoke as though this was something she might expect, rather than a bolt from the blue, and as he did, he was looking towards the top of her head.

Zillah nodded but still no words came. As much as she wanted to take Reg's part, he and her mother would have to sort this one out. It was difficult enough to get herself to a chair near her mother and take a seat.

Alice had made a pot of tea so Zillah poured herself a cup slowly, hoping that the muscles on her face did not give anything away. The milk jug was in front of Reg and she debated having her tea black to avoid asking him to pass it, in case she got eye contact and it tempted him to wink at her or give a sign that they knew each other well. In her confusion, she stood without meaning to and leaned in front of him to get the jug. If her mother had noticed the rude behaviour, she said nothing.

Her mum was doing most of the talking, filling in the gaps around Reg's strained, short bursts of words, rounding them up like a well-trained sheepdog that had been tied up for days and finally had the chance to get a flock through the gate. After some minutes, the conversation turned to last season's premiership win. Zillah's brothers must have been impressed when they got home after the game because Alice knew about Reg's third goal, which had put Waratah four points ahead to take out the flag from the Rovers.

As they talked about the game, Reg relaxed back in the chair and unfolded one leg a little to the side. The conversation moved seamlessly on to the difficulty in getting the numbers to keep four teams going, the lack of work for young men in the district and what a disgrace it was that Magnet's silver mine was likely to close soon.

"So, these days, the leg's not too good," Zillah heard him saying, suddenly aware that she had been stirring the milky tea so intently she'd stopped listening.

"She had the willow leg done in Melbourne back in '19 and it was good at first, but the stump's giving her a lot of pain these days."

Alice remembered now, the widow with the same name as her, doing it tough, with two boys who'd been to war. How the sports clubs and others had run raffles and dances and collected gate-takings to raise money for the artificial leg. Diabetes, wasn't it? She didn't read the newspaper much but it seemed like every time she'd opened it there had been an advertisement for Mrs Sutton's Fund, a rallying cry for the community to do something good after the evil of the war that ended the year before.

"Yeah, I try to keep her spirits up as much as I can, especially now most of the others are married and gone," Reg said. The words might easily have sounded saintly or contrived but instead they were gravel falling heavily into the room, leaving an echo around the three of them at the table.

Over the next few minutes, Zillah saw something she had never believed could be possible. To her astonishment, her mother changed her mind.

"Alright then, I suppose Zillah can go to Burnie for a night but she has to be back first thing Friday mind. And drive carefully."

Reg had been winded more than once on the football field so if the about turn landed a blow, he didn't show it. He picked up his hat from the table, thanked Alice politely then turned to Zillah, who was deliberately quiet to mask her excitement.

"I'll pick you up at three o'clock tomorrow then. Mum'll be looking forward to it."

Zillah was still at a loss for words long after the front door had squeaked shut.

7

They were on their way to Burnie, winding down the last couple of hairpin bends to the myrtle-swept river at the bottom of Hellyer Gorge when Reg, one hand on the steering wheel of the hire car, finally told her he was leaving Waratah.

"Wait, you mean next week?"

For the second time in recent days, she wondered whether there was some special code or language she ought to learn; she often seemed unable to know what others were thinking. Not the children, she knew where they were at, but the adults could be impossible to fathom.

"Yair. There's nothing more for me to do for Ray and he can't afford to keep me on. Besides, I can't keep staying in Cyril's room."

Zillah had assumed that when his bar job had finished he would eventually pick up another job in town. She hadn't counted on there being nothing more after Reg's casual role was done.

He sounded cool, resigned to the need to go, quite unlike the hot-headedness and determination the night she had refused his proposal.

"What will you do?" The novelty of going for a drive with him faded, like the road disappearing behind them as they crossed the bridge.

"Dunno. Guess I'll look for work on the coast,

though some fellas have said there's money to be had on the mainland in the Red Centre. They reckon there's gold to be found out of Alice Springs around Tennant Creek and at least it'd be hot there."

Zillah wanted to cry, to beg him to stay. But she was the one who couldn't marry and she wasn't ready for another round of that voice of hers saying things even she could not predict. She looked out the window for a long while. The only sounds were the tyres singing something mournful and the clicking of the Chev's floor shift as they climbed up from the river.

She turned to him, searching for some hope. "They reckon they'll start building the Burnie paper mill in a year or so and there'll be plenty of jobs there. If you're on the coast, we could still see each other sometimes."

"We could, darling girl, we could."

"You don't sound so sure, Reg."

"It's not just about what I'll do till then, and who knows if they'll even get started on the mill for years? It's about us and how it's going to work if I can't marry you, be with you. It'd be impossible if I'm living somewhere else to turn up and be sneaking around so we can spend time together."

He was right, of course. Since he'd proposed, she'd been trying hard to believe it would all go on the same. In a way it had been easy to let herself enjoy the moments she was with him and not think about the future.

"Why are you taking me to your mother's, then?" Odd, how the question hadn't occurred to her before.

"She knows I've been seeing you and I want her to find out for herself why you're so special to me. Maybe you'll feel differently after you spend a bit of time with her and meet Owen, or any of the others if they're around."

So it wasn't about cheering up his mother. She smiled at him, caught in the pleasure of him wanting to show her off. Maybe that was enough for now and they could work the rest out later, a way to stay in touch, to still be friends if she dared not be his wife. Kathleen, for all her irritating childishness at times, was right. She was going to have to deal with Reg and where their friendship might go, one way or another, but not today when it was so delicious being in the car and away from Waratah, going somewhere with a man who cared about her.

They emerged from the gorge and its trees packed cheek by jowl and soon were dipping through spreading green pastures and paddocks where ploughs had churned up red, iron-rich soil that once had been volcanic rock. There was no need for further conversation and they continued the journey in a comfortable silence.

The kitchen at the weatherboard house in Wilmot Street was at the rear, the same as Zillah's home. She was nervous when Reg introduced her to Alice, whose face showed the lines and craters left by the rough passage of life though was capable of a warm smile regardless. She settled, however, when her offer to help do the potatoes for tea was accepted.

"You can put your suitcase in the girls' old room before we get started." Zillah followed her into the passageway, where two doors opened on either side. They turned left into the first one and she sat her small tan case on the closest of the two single beds, both pushed against a wall with a small rug separating them.

Back in the kitchen, Zillah kept her eyes firmly on the pearly white innards of the Bismarks as she peeled and cut them. It was a way to hold back the impulse to stare at Alice's stiff, awkward gait between the table and the bench as she shifted her weight from the good leg to the wooden one with painful purpose.

"It gets to me some days. I don't care what the doctor says, it hurts worse where the leg used to be than it does with what I've got left." Though Alice winced as she spoke, Zillah was glad the subject was out in the open.

"Not easy, Mum. At least you can still get around," Reg said.

Owen came home and while they all sat around and ate, Zillah found herself slipping easily into banter with the boys, just as she did with her brothers at the tea table at home. While Zillah was helping gather up the dishes after the meal, Owen announced he was off to the pub.

"You comin', Reg? I'm just going down to the Club Hotel for the one. Harry said he could let a few of us in through the back, now they've got the new sergeant in their pocket."

Reg smiled knowingly at Owen, who never left a pub with much less than a skinful. He looked to Zillah, who glanced quickly at Alice but then nodded. "You go, Reg. I'm happy to have a cuppa and a chat with your mum."

Alice wasn't so sure about her boys drinking in a bar after closing time yet again. "How many fines do you two need!" She shook her head, her mouth stretched tight and straight.

Owen flashed his mother a winning smile in reply, immediately tipping his head towards Reg then gesturing to the back door.

"Won't be long. We have to be on the road fairly early in the morning 'cos I need to get you home on time." Reg winked at Zillah then tumbled out the door behind Owen, throwing his jacket over his shoulder as they left.

Half-a-dozen men gathered in the bar, where only one of the lights had been left on, and they kept the noise down out of respect for the barman extending them the favour of a private drinking session. They were all men Reg had known for most of his life but he and Owen were the only two not married.

"Must be about time you got hitched. Time's running out, you know. The good ones are all getting taken," one of them levelled at Reg.

Owen's gob was open before Reg got the chance to jam it shut with a glare.

"Oh, he's workin' on it, don't you worry," Owen laughed, enjoying the chance to score a point.

Reg moved fast to divert the conversation before he got any tricky questions and, fortunately for him, Owen felt he'd already gotten one up on Reg and did not resist.

After a few beers, Reg gave Owen the slip, going in the direction of the toilet but instead leaving quietly to run back through the town centre, not caring if any blokes he knew might see him, so he could catch some time with Zillah. When he got in, his mother was sitting alone at the table, the newspaper spread out in front of her.

"You just missed her. She went to bed about half an hour ago," Alice said, without looking up.

Reg shut the door and sat down opposite her. "Well, what do you think, Mum? Do you like her?"

Alice closed the newspaper and sighed out a long breath. "She's a lovely, bright girl, Reg, and a hard worker. There's no denying that, and she's keen on her family, which is a good thing. But she was talking about her mum and that woman's Irish through to her shoe leather. They're all Micks and you know how they feel about people like us, no matter how much time we spend on our knees."

Reg was studying his mother, listening to what was an uncommonly long commentary from her, and aware she was still winding up.

"What are you thinking, boy? This is never going to go anywhere and I don't know why you're bothering to get yourself so attached to a girl that in the end you're never going to be able to marry. Besides, she'd have to go against her mother and I hardly think that's going to make for a happy life for her or for you."

Reg hadn't expected his mother to be so forthright and certainly not so definite. He picked idly at a small scab near one of the knuckles on his left hand, sorry now that he had brought Zillah home. He'd been hoping his mother would approve, would encourage him to keep going after such a wonderful girl, might even help him to talk the family at Waratah around.

"She's worth it, Mum. She says she'd marry me if her mother was onside. I'm not giving up, I gotta figure out a way to make it work." He was getting angry, partly because he hated the way he was sounding more like a five-year-old in a tantrum than a grown man but especially because for the past couple of weeks he'd felt cast adrift and his mother was the one supposed to throw the lifebuoy.

"No use getting snarky with me, Reg. Someone's

got to tell you the cold, hard truth. Yes, she's terrific but she's not going to stand up to her mother. There'll be other girls who'll make you a good wife, it's not the end of the world." Her voice softened and she reached over and patted him on the arm.

He laid his hand over hers briefly and looked down so she wouldn't see his eyes were moist. "Yeah, I guess," he said, knowing full well that a speech like that meant it was her final word.

They sat for a while, quiet together, listening to the old house creaking on its bones as it settled for the night. "Well, best get some kip. Goodnight." He left her gathering up an armful of kindling from the back porch to put in front of the stove ready for morning.

He went to the bedroom off the verandah. After he stripped to his singlet and underpants, it seemed like too much effort to swing his legs onto the bed and he sat on the edge for a long time, his head sagging in his hands. He was acutely aware that Zillah, the clever, smiling girl of his heart, was in the room next door yet the longer he sat there, turning flesh into stone, the further away she seemed to get.

Next morning, Friday, they said their goodbyes early and Reg drove around the corner and along North Terrace to West Beach. He left the car on the street near the Beach Hotel, where his brother had a room, though it was too early for Allan to be behind the bar. They waited for a shunting loco to pass on its way to the wharf then crossed the railway line to the surf club, facing north into the bay. To the right of them, the sea heaved itself onto boulders protecting the Marine Board offices at Blackman Point and smashed against the seawall for Ocean Pier, pumping spray high into the air. Zillah could taste the salt from where she stood on the concrete ramp beside the clubhouse.

Reg slipped his hand in hers and she leaned in, her shoulder against his arm, while he talked about what it was like to be out there, stroke after stroke, working with the force of a sea where the currents of the Indian Ocean from the west met the power of the Tasman Sea from the east and could, in an instant, turn deadly.

"It's a funny feeling, once you get out past the point and you're looking at that horizon, 'cos it feels like it would be so easy to go out to meet the sky and keep going to Melbourne.

"In your head, you know it's more than two hundred miles over the strait to the mainland but the sea feels like a big, bucking animal and you're riding on its back and it's carrying you along. And you just want to go with it and see if you can stay on it to the end."

Zillah's gaze had drifted towards the western end of the beach, where the new brick high school dwarfed Parsonage Point. But there was something in his longing that made her head snap back. She looked directly at him.

"Reg, there's been hundreds of shipwrecks between here and the mainland and there were four hundred people or more, babies and all, died on just one of them that went down near King Island," she said, barely drawing breath. She knew she was getting worked up and was battling to rein herself in, the words tumbling faster and her voice growing shrill.

"The water out there's bigger and more dangerous than the English Channel and you'd be a fool to even think about swimming it."

It was a relief when he roared with laughter and reached up to tweak her nose, enjoying the turn of events because he was usually the one getting in a lather. She bumped her hip against him playfully and, encouraged by the gesture, he snatched a quick kiss then led her back to the black sedan.

They said little on the trip back to Waratah but for different reasons. Zillah scooted across the car seat to be close to Reg, not wanting to chase away this new feeling that wrapped around her chest and slowed the blood in her veins. *Yes*, she thought, *this is contentment*. Right now I am finally feeling what it is to be full and happy with what I have. Anything else can wait until tomorrow.

Beside her, Reg gripped the steering wheel with both hands and fixed his eyes on the dirt road parting thick rainforest and leading them back down the West Coast. A thought perched on the edge of his awareness, lacking form but waiting, alert for any crumbs he might toss in its direction that could provide a hint of sustenance for it to grow and take shape. It had first shown up when he was standing with her, hand in hand, at the beach and it had been easy to send it away then. He was a powerful swimmer, not afraid to face into the might of the sea, yet this half-something wanting to speak to him was cause for every instinct to say no. No, go the other way.

When he pulled over in front of her house, she took her time getting out, not ready to leave the cocoon of closeness and quiet connection she'd felt sitting beside him on the journey. As she stood on the running board and leaned back into the car to say goodbye, she thought he looked sad. The light in his eyes had retreated, even as he held her gaze while she pushed the door shut between them.

She greeted her mother then went to her room, and was halfway through unpacking her suitcase before she heard him drive away.

Reg stayed at Waratah all weekend, mainly because Zillah was going to the fundraising dance on the Saturday night at St James's Anglican Church hall and it was a chance to hold her in his arms. But he had not expected her mother to be there.

"Not every dance, Reg. She'll be watching," Zillah whispered in his ear as he got her up for the Gypsy Tap, uncomfortable because it was new on the program and most of the older dancers were sitting it out.

He hung about for most of the Monday morning, April Fool's Day. Before lunch, Jean was playing with a friend when she noticed him partially hidden by the remains of a hawthorn hedge in the nearby vacant block and watching the front of the Camp Road house. It was something Jean had seen him do before and soon she turned her attention back to the game of hopscotch on the verandah.

Soon after, Reg drove back to Burnie. He had a beer at the Beach Hotel, chatting quietly to Allan while his brother got things in hand for the after-work droves. It was an effort to be talking without saying anything, straining from his jaw to his toes to achieve an impression of ease. His left hand was in a ball on his lap but he registered that the right one, in full view on the bar, was clenched and he released the fingers, lifting them to the glass in an attempt to cradle the beer rather than giving in to the urge to seize it. He was grateful for the cold glass, a small anchor to steady him in a room with walls that dissolved on the edges of his vision. Even the blunt stool beneath him seemed fragile and not quite there.

It was his brother on the other side of the bar, for Chrissake, moving in a well-practised dance of bending down, reaching up, stepping forward then back, mapping something solid. It was his brother, his eyes were telling him, but his brain wasn't recognising any truth in it and he was aware of a gap opening between him and the bar and its sounds. The strange quality of separation set off a panic in his gut that was uncomfortable, yet it was tinged with what might be relief because at least he was feeling something.

"How's it going looking for other work?" Allan asked, reaching around to lift a tray of clean beer glasses from the drainer on the sink.

"Yeah okay, not much out there but you never know," Reg replied, his voice deliberately casual so Allan didn't suspect he'd given up on the idea of getting work anywhere.

His brother disappeared into the storeroom, returning with extra ashtrays and a loss of interest in further conversation. Reg was relieved and drank the rest of his beer undisturbed.

About 2 pm he strode up Wilson Street to Ivey's chemist shop and walked up to the counter, where pharmacist Ernest West greeted him and inquired after his mother.

"She's not bad, all things considering. Thanks for asking." Reg pulled a handful of coins from his pocket. "How much for strychnine?" he asked the chemist.

"Five shillings for an ounce, three for half an ounce."

"I reckon half an ounce is enough," Reg said, counting out the money.

Ernest held up a hand, palm facing Reg. "Sorry, I

can't sell it to you without a witness. It's the law, I'm afraid."

Reg dropped the money back in his pocket, nodded his thanks and left the shop. Ten minutes later, he was coming back through the doorway with his friend, Reg Spinks, who was asking, "What do you need it for, anyway?"

"I've got shell shock," Reg told him, tossing back his head for a hearty laugh before composing himself. "Nah, rabbits, lots of rabbits."

The two friends not only shared the same first name and football team, they'd trained together as surf life-saving instructors and their talk quickly strayed to sport. "With more blokes leaving, we're gonna need a couple more players to keep up our winning streak this season," his mate lamented, leaning against the counter.

They signed the register and Reg paid the assistant, all the while yarning to his friend, while Ernest went out the back to organise the label for the bottle of crystals. When he came back, Reg pocketed the small, brown bottle and the two friends left the shop. His mate turned to go.

"Better get the rest of the supplies or I'll be late leaving for Waratah and Dad'll be at the bakery ready to give me a right ol' chewing over. Maybe have a beer later in the week?" They shook hands and parted ways.

About an hour later, Reg was also on the road to

Waratah. It was only when he was driving the hire car past the sawmill at Parrawe, along the damp patch of road where a dense canopy of old myrtles formed a leafy tunnel that blocked the sun, that he remembered Zillah and her sister Isobel were staying the night with their friends, the Fagan girls.

It was about 5 pm when he pulled up in front of the Bischoff Hotel and got out, waving to Cyril, who had seen him through the bar window. Inside, it was the bedlam hour and local workers were hard at it, downing as many beers as they could before service stopped at 6 pm. Cyril didn't get a chance to glance back out the window till after the bar had closed and when he did, the car was gone.

Questioned later, Cyril admitted he thought it a bit odd, as was the story Reg told him the next day when he got back from Burnie, about how he'd been stuck with the car in the Hellyer Gorge and had to get petrol from the dentist, Mr Wells.

Cyril had still been pouring beers and the street-lights in Camp Road had been flickering on when Reg pointed the squat nose of the sedan up the straight that led towards Burnie, working the floor shift intently and gunning the motor as he passed the town boundary sign and the lone cypress planted by an earlier resident in a more hopeful time. He dipped down to the bridge and took the left-hand corner so fast the car shook and skidded over to the wrong side of the road. On the next straight, he wound up the Chev to its top speed but by the time the needle hit 65 miles per hour, he was forced to pump the brakes for a series of sweeping corners.

Reg wasn't much concerned about where he was going, it was the road that mattered and being on the road, letting it take him this way and that, dropping down at the Fingerpost turn-off then climbing again. All he had to do was watch the twin beams of yellow light, pulling him into the darkness with no need for decisions or plans, along the path laid out ahead.

He had tried so hard to see into next week, next month, next year and now, his hands on the wheel feeling the bump of small potholes, the soft shudder in the corners, the car responding smoothly and strongly as he powered through, it was a bloody good thing to be free of thinking. All he needed to know was in front of him, the light showing the way and the darkness taking every damn thing he didn't need.

He drove on like that for several more miles and soon he was slowing as he entered the steep gorge section and its long series of hairpin bends. The Chev crisscrossed its way down the side of the ravine and when he got to the rest area at the bridge, he turned in for no reason at all. At the far end of the clearing, he cut the motor and the lights and rolled the window down an inch or two. The river was keening low and steady over its rocky bed and, above the rush of water, he could hear the rasping and hissing of a couple of possums screaming nasty filth about territory.

Ripe smells of damp leaf litter and mossy grass hung heavily in the stillness. As his eyes adjusted, the silhouette of the rainforest emerged soft against a clear, starry sky. It could all go to hell, he thought, the whole sorry lot out there beyond the bush and the heart bashing away in his chest. He would rest here a while and maybe go on to Burnie or somewhere else.

He reached under the seat for the bottle he'd jammed there earlier in the day and took his time unscrewing the lid. The first slug of whisky was a double punch: ice on his tongue then fire in his throat and belly. He snatched at air with lips parted wide and took another mouthful before resting his head back, his limbs softening into the leather seat.

Soon his thoughts stirred so he drank again—two big gulps that went down easily, followed by some more. He pressed the cold bottle against his forehead, his head bowed. May the grace of our Lord Jesus Christ and the love of God, and the fellowship of the Holy Spirit be with us all, now and ever more. Amen. The words recited automatically, like all those times he sat in church as a child, never feeling the blessing in their intention, not then and not now.

Slumped there on the seat with time suspended, it was not the whisky but another bottle that called to him and offered more. He pulled it out of the glove box and held it in his hand, his fingers wrapping around its curves, the bottle weighing almost nothing at all. Soon, it was warm and comfortable there in his palm.

What would it take to remove the cap, shake one or two of the tiny, potent crystals into his hand and toss it back with a mouthful of firewater? In less than a moment it would be done, so swift there in the purple-blue night that any threshold would have no time to thicken, no chance to be a marker and to say, "Look, it's before, and look, now it's after". Everything would dissolve into one merging trick of time and space, melting the aching in his lungs and bones and taking him away, past any horizon.

He swigged more whisky and other thoughts came too, his resistance weakening with every mouthful of the burning liquid, the voices tumbling freely now that he had no will to hold them back. Round and round they went as the hours passed.

The thoughts, oh Jesus they hurt. Such burning pain from his own bloody mind, clawing at his flesh, hammering at his heart, piercing lungs and liver worse than if he took to them with the long narrow blade of his fishing knife. A personal, bloodied hell stormed out from his centre to flood his chest and belly. This force rising up and shaking him to the core was real and he heard the howl long before he realised it came from his own throat, the tortured sound of knowing that he had wasted all that time shoring up the barricades when there was never a chance he could hold any of it back.

In the deepest blackness before dawn, he passed out and did not stir until the mail lorry thrashed down through its gears to the bridge then groaned and clanked up the other side. Coming to, it was his neck he registered first, and he worked at it for a while before he could straighten the sharp angle where it had dropped to the left. As he raised his head, unkinking his neck, the trapped nerves responded immediately by radiating waves of a particular sensation. There was a name for it and he was grasping at dirty air that he didn't yet know was his breath then at a string of useless words that shot up through the fog in his brain. By the time he had badged it as pain, it was too late. The waves were rolling out to join others coming from who knows where and they crashed together in one mighty triumph of turbulence that ricocheted through his skull.

The agony propelled him out of the car and as he lurched forward, the small bottle fell to the ground. His hand shot out and he followed the bottle down to catch it and, as he did, his ribs made a savage attack on his stomach and his eyes seemed to spin in their sockets. He went to swear but the effort nearly throttled him and he leaned clumsily against the car before falling back through the open door and thumping onto the seat. So damn tired; heavy with hauling his own life through the days behind him and exhausted at the idea of hauling it through the days ahead.

He sat there, not moving, for a long time and it was only the need for a smoke that roused him. He searched with the least movement he could muster, reaching over to the back seat for the new pack of cigarettes tossed there the day before.

Christ, he couldn't even get his knees to bend properly. He rocked like a wind-up bloody toy to get to the edge of the picnic area but the effort was worth it because he had to escape the vile fug in the Chev and he was desperate for a piss. Afterwards, he had a smoke and then a second, waiting for the buzz from the nicotine and the hit of cold morning air to do their work.

The horror of the hangover was closing in yet below it, as he flicked the fag end into the bush, he felt a small bubble of calm rising up. He could see through its flimsy membrane and what he saw snapped his spine upright.

Gawd, he had it all wrong. He'd been working with the pieces of a puzzle, straining and forcing them this past month because he thought if he tried hard enough he could knock them into shape. Each piece holding out, feigning knowledge and power but fighting back until now, when his struggle reached an end. In the moment that he emptied out, it happened just like scattered stars drawing forward in a night sky to punch out the shape of the Southern Cross. A spark lit up and hot-wired his brain, telegraphing one clear, fully formed idea.

Later, down at the river, he could feel his skin all stiff like a calico sugar bag, only instead of sweet whiteness it was filled with his bones. He crouched slowly, carefully, for fear he would set off again the painful pulsing in his head, and held his right hand in the rushing mountain water until his fingers went numb. When he could no longer feel his hand, he watched on as though another man's arm was working in front of him and he had no part in it.

The hand began with the small bottle in his left palm, fingers bending to the task of washing the two labels off the glass. First went the small one with the word "strychnine" and the antidote, which took a while because there was a string of fine black print. Then the hand rubbed away the chemist's name, the date and weight of the contents. The second label was easy because most of it came away in one lumpy gob as the glue broke down. Finally, the fingernails scratched away the skull and crossbones printed at the bottom.

8

While Reg crouched by the river, getting ready to drive back to Waratah, Zillah and her friend Maggie were leafing through the autumn mail order catalogue, keeping up a steady critique of the latest Melbourne fashions. Isobel had gone home, which was welcome because they could give their opinions freely without facing any eye-rolling or harrumphing from the only one of the trio who'd actually been to the Myer Emporium.

While Maggie sometimes had money to send off for a new blouse or shoes, Zillah did not but it in no way diminished her enthusiasm for what was on offer. This was a favourite pastime and she could happily keep at it for hours.

"Thirteen shillings," squealed Maggie, pointing to her favourite, a calf-length blue dress with a big collar and a narrow belt showing off a neat waist. Zillah looked over her friend's shoulder and wondered how all the women in the illustrations seemed so easy in their flowing elegance and pointed shoes. When she wore heels her toes felt pinched and her ankles ached for more practical footwear, so how did they do it? And, especially, where did they go in their stylish suits and coats?

She hadn't even been to Launceston, let alone a huge city like Melbourne with its vast theatres, lively dance halls, trams and so many shops it was impossible to imagine how you could ever get around them all. Sometimes late at night when she couldn't sleep, she lay there and pretended she wasn't in a dirty mining town but in her own cosy bedsit in Melbourne. When she woke, she would step into a fitted suit and leave for the office and her own desk and telephone. After work, she would go out with the other secretaries to drink martinis and listen to a band. She would answer to no-one. Her mother snoring in the bedroom opposite or Jean mumbling in her sleep would inevitably pierce the fantasy.

Her nocturnal imaginings were not something to share with Maggie, whose father had more wealth than most in Waratah, giving her at least some hope of achieving her dreams. Zillah wasn't jealous of this fact and would have kept speculating about new clothes she would never wear and the woman she might become, but for the knowledge that her mother would be waiting.

She farewelled Maggie and left to buy apples. As she hurried towards the main street, she let out a grunt without meaning to. There was always something on the list of things to do and as fast as she ticked them off her mum was busy adding more chores. At least at the fruit and vegetable shop she had a laugh, getting the special treat of arriving just before the phone rang in the adjoining general store. She and her friends never tired of the entertaining spectacle of Bill Shady, the proprietor, running to get his hat and carefully placing it on his head before picking up the receiver to speak.

She couldn't see Reg's hire car in the street but thought maybe he'd parked at the back of the pub. After two days he was on her mind and it was a new feeling, but she had come to the conclusion that she was missing him. She would take a walk this evening, she decided, to see if he was about. She made sure she was home in time for dinner with her mother at noon so she could get the flatiron heating on the woodstove while they ate, ready for an afternoon of smoothing out the wrinkles and creases in school uniforms, shirts, football shorts, pillowslips and tablecloths.

"This would be a lot quicker if we had an electric iron," she said, lifting the heavy iron from the stove and spitting on it to make sure it was hot enough.

"You saying it every week is not making it any more likely to happen," her mother snapped back, buttoning up her coat before leaving to visit her unwell sister.

Zillah toiled on and by the time her mother returned in the late afternoon, the clothes were in neat piles and she was packing up the ironing board. Her mother was in a good mood and seemed pleased with her handiwork. When Zillah told her she would eat at the Kellys', Alice told her she could leave the clothes to her and she would put them away.

"Don't forget Kathleen's coming back here tonight. We'll be back after tea," Zillah called from the passageway, rushing out in case her mother changed her mind and made her stay to finish the job.

The Kelly mob was a noisy lot and they were in full voice as Zillah walked in. Kathleen immediately grabbed her by the elbow and steered her out to the chook shed, slowly being swallowed by twilight.

"Well, how'd it go?" she hissed close to her friend's ear. This was their first private moment since Zillah's return from Burnie with Reg.

The racket in the house carried out to them on the damp air and Zillah decided this wasn't something she wanted to get into right now, partly because there could be a distraction at any moment but mainly because she still hadn't decided how much to share with Kathleen. The Greeks knew that Eros was a kind of madness sent by the gods and what she had begun feeling with Reg seemed more akin with their beings than the Catholic one that waited for her in church.

She felt light-headed and excited but there was also something about him that niggled. He was good to her; when they were together he listened and was attentive and she found herself opening up to him more and more, though she held the line at kissing and hand-holding because she was never going to be one of those wayward girls her mother talked about with such venom.

She shuddered. It hadn't been that long ago and her mother had been full of it. That poor girl, her own age, who'd gone out of the district for work and come back to live with her parents, barely able to button up her skirt and abandoned by her lover. She'd been the talk of the town but as the months went by, the prospect of an illegitimate child turned out to be a lesser evil. No-one had seen a baby, which was strange in such a small place, but the explanation was in plain view at the inquest and the Supreme Court hearing.

The girl had given birth in her bed unassisted and afterwards, exhausted, had slept for a few hours. She woke to find the newborn stiff and blue beside her, and with no memory of what had happened. In a panic, she'd wrapped the baby in a shawl and walked at dawn towards the Mount Bischoff mine, hiding the body in scrub and covering it with branches to deter scavenging Tasmanian devils that might see it as a meal. She was gaoled for three months for concealing the birth of a child. Zillah, remembering the tender burst of care as she took her day-old sister in her arms a decade earlier, had thought the girl was already punished enough.

She was careful with Reg on their walks in the dark, not letting things go too far, though the kissing had gone well past a couple of awkward experiments with local lads. Maybe the stab of anxiety that pierced the attraction was about her lack of experience with men. Had she been willing to risk criticism and confide in her sister, she might have found a way to capture a description for the uncomfortable feeling. When she was with him, he made himself her whole world and she was a country within it, a living landmass hitched to him. Sometimes though she wanted to break away, to put an ocean between them for a while, but then would scold herself because, after all, this was how it was when you were serious about somebody.

As Zillah stood there with Kathleen, she felt there was much she needed to pin down for herself and she didn't want to speak and have it come out all wrong with her impressionable confidante.

"Yeah, good. I'll tell you about it later at my place," she whispered, hoping to sound convincing.

Kathleen stamped her foot playfully and pouted. "Zillah, I've already waited since Friday. That's really not fair. I wouldn't do that to you." But before she could push a little harder, they were called back into the house to eat.

At the Kellys', the unspoken rule was that visitors, even regular ones who were almost part of the family, were exempt from doing the dishes. Zillah and her friend slipped away soon after the meal was over and followed the road towards Waratah, stepping arm in arm under a thin lick of moon.

Back at home, Zillah tried to sit and talk with the others but found herself pacing, looking for tasks that might cover her inability to be still. Before her mother scolded her for being in the way, she cornered Kathleen and announced, a little too brightly, that they were going for a bit of a walk.

Kathleen, who'd just settled in, knew what the walk was about but saw it as an opportunity to continue her questioning and break through her friend's stonewalling. As they headed down Camp Road towards the centre of town, Kathleen was careful as she circled the conversation back around and got ready to pounce. So she wasn't impressed when, walking towards the hall, they met Reg.

She drifted behind them as far as the station and a bit before eight o'clock, tired of feeling in the way, left the two lovebirds and went back to Camp Road, full of resolve to get the whole story when Zillah got home. She was almost asleep when Zillah sneaked into the bedroom about half past nine, saying little as she changed into a nightie and slid into the other end of the single bed.

Kathleen grumbled about the cold feet beside her shoulder but soon dozed off to the sound of her friend's low, steady voice. At some stage, a string of words or maybe it was their desperate tone tugged at her, calling her back from the shallows of sleep. Things had been difficult with Reg, Kathleen understood that much, and there was something more, delivered in a whisper; something Reg had said that seemed to bother Zillah. Kathleen registered the words but any meaning melted into the fog that had overtaken her brain and, try as she might, she couldn't haul herself back to the wakefulness needed to make sense of them.

Next morning, Kathleen was up early and keen to hear what Zillah had shared but her friend was already in the kitchen, helping with breakfast. The two women agreed to meet after chores for blackberry picking and Kathleen headed back to Magnet Junction about seven o'clock, satisfied that she would get the full story later.

Zillah went into the paddock at the rear of the house and tied up the old Jersey in the cow bail, hooking a second rope around her back leg because she had a nasty habit of kicking forward and knocking over the milk bucket. She wasn't enjoying doing things with Kathleen the way she used to and she couldn't deny the fact any longer. Their time together was starting to seem childish and she was the one who needed to grow up and be more of a woman, though the idea of a life like her mother's was as welcome as a knife in the back.

She had to face it, she was changing and it was scary to see how little she could do to stop it. Her belly, her arms and legs—when she looked down they no longer seemed to fit and it was a weird feeling. Sometimes she had the strange thought that maybe she wasn't even here at all.

The change had started before Reg came on the scene, she could see that now. As she'd been getting on with things, in some far corner a speck of grit had found its way into her spirit and the chafing had begun. Then he arrived with his attention and the promise of a life where she might stand at the centre. What had been irritation, easy to dismiss, had turned into a magnetic field, only it was not iron filings that were sticking but all manner of unease that was unfamiliar.

Not knowing who she was becoming or how it would be was rattling her. And then there was the business of her future with Reg and not wanting to upset her mother, but she couldn't let him go either. Surely a path would open; there must be a way forward.

She usually liked the time with the cow in the quiet yard, resting her head on the warm flanks and settling into the rhythm of milking, patient as her fingers loosened up to find that sweet spot where each squeeze–pull on the teats from one hand then the other drew out a steady flow of steaming liquid. Today, though, she leaned away from the cow so the Jersey's weight didn't add to the pressure shrinking her scalp.

The cow knew it was different and turned her long orange-brown face, a white patch circling one calm brown eye, to nuzzle in with her wet nose. As the big face gave a nod, Zillah shook her head despite herself and chuckled. It was hard to keep up the worrying when only a few inches away were those giant eyelashes, perfect without the messy business of fiddling with a damp brush and a cake of mascara.

Back in the house, she boiled up the milk and had just finished skimming it when her brothers came lumbering into the kitchen. They piled jam on their toast before she dropped dollops of warm cream that ran in trails through blackberry stickiness.

Zillah brushed Jean's unruly red curls while her sister grumbled about how it didn't matter that she was now ten years old if she still wasn't allowed to have her hair cut short. The boys rolled their eyes and ignored her complaints and after Zillah had helped preparing the lunches, they left for work. Jean lingered till the last possible moment, racing off in time to beat the headmaster's bell.

While her mother sorted dirty clothes, Zillah went out to the woodshed. The dry wood was stacked against the side wall and she grabbed the smallest piece, shaving off thin shards with the tomahawk to start a hot fire under the copper. In her haste, she split a fat grub hiding along the grain where rot had set in. The two halves curled pitifully in the woodchips, powdered with dust.

It was almost half past ten by the time Zillah had

done the breakfast wash-up, swept the kitchen and got the copper boiling so her mother could have a clear go at a big day of washing. She cut herself a hasty sandwich from leftover corned beef and packed it in the billycan, hurrying to get out the door so she could catch Reg before she met her friend.

"Don't worry if I'm not home by half past four, Mum. I might stay at Kathleen's for tea," she called over her shoulder as she grabbed the bucket from the porch on the way out. Her glance caught Alice in the act of heaving sodden clothes from the viciously hot water, swinging them on an old broom handle towards the wringer. Zillah grinned. A middle-aged demon summoning heat and steam, definitely not something she would dare say out loud. Alice, for her part, did not look up.

At the Bischoff Hotel, Reg's day had started early, too. He thought he'd tossed some spare change into the dented brown suitcase a few days ago, but when he lifted the lid his shoulders drooped: the sixpence in the corner wasn't even worth bending down for. "Anyway, it doesn't matter," he muttered to himself, then began whistling with the energy of a man who'd slept for a solid eight hours, even though he had not. "A beer and breakfast it is."

As he entered the bar at 8.30 am, he saw Cyril taking great pains to wipe down the countertop, making sure there was no room for complaint when the publican, Ray Whyman, a canny former packman who had made his money ferrying supplies in mud and mess on the early mining fields, turned his sharp eyes to the quality of the cleaning work.

"You had breakfast yet?" Reg asked Cyril.

"No, but I could eat the crotch out of a low-flying duck," Cyril thundered.

"Righto. I'll have a drink while I wait for you."

Reg was well into his second glass of ale when Cyril finished setting up for opening time. In the dining room, they asked for eggs and bacon and tucked in, elbows working fast as they demolished their breakfast. Cyril did most of the talking but he thought nothing of it; he knew that Reg had a lot on his mind with the work coming to an end.

As they left the room, Reg called out to the girls in the kitchen: "I'll come back in a minute and give you a hand with the washing up."

He followed Cyril back to the bar and sat there while his roommate worked, lingering over another beer. Then he eased himself off the stool and left to help with the breakfast dishes.

Cyril was ready to open the bar door when Reg returned a few minutes before ten o'clock. They had a drink together, Cyril hastily downing a beer and Reg lingering over a whisky, before Reg bought a bottle of Boag's Special Ale and a pack of cigarettes.

"The rail motor'll be in from Guildford soon.

Might take the men down a drink," he said. Cyril put the tall bottle of ale into a brown paper bag and handed it across the bar.

Reg threw back another whisky. "Do you mind if I borrow a glass?"

In other circumstances it might have seemed like an odd request but Cyril's attention was on the early drinkers straggling in the door and he was looking in their direction as he nodded. Reg took an empty whisky glass from the shelf above the bar.

"See you later," he called over his shoulder as he sauntered out the door, shoving the nip glass into the bag with the beer.

"Not excited, just his usual self," Cyril would say when questioned later in the week.

As Reg stepped out onto the footpath, he was met by the steady thud-thud of the stamper batteries pounding the tributers' raw ore to dust in the sheds, a series of stick insects clad in corrugated iron, perched down the side of the valley. No matter how many times he left the town and returned, the sound always took him by surprise, especially the way it seemed to rise out of nowhere, close at hand yet strangely out of reach. You knew the source was there below the grassy bank—you could count the simple one-two beat—yet there were no visible signs or movement. He liked the idea of that; it comforted him as he walked towards the station with no intention of meeting the rail motor.

Michael Donovan, recently transferred back to Waratah after a promotion to constable-in-charge, was striding up from the police station about eleven o'clock as the snub-nosed passenger vehicle came in from Burnie. It was approaching the platform when he caught sight of Reg, crossing from the footpath to the railway line.

Whenever he thought about that moment in the days to come, he remembered his old sergeant training him the first year after he got his constable's badge. The rant was the same every time they returned from a break-in, an assault, a burglary or an accident: "Powers of observation, lad, that's what you gotta have. You've got to pay attention to the facts, the details—what's in front of your bloody nose is never what you first think". He would slam his fist on the desk, rattling all forty-four keys on the Remington, which may have been why it never typed evenly from one report to the next.

In the ordinariness of the moment and his eagerness to get the package with his new boots, the last thing on his mind was the sergeant's code. As Donovan walked towards the station platform, he glanced at the brown paper parcel under the footballer's right arm.

"Morning Reg," he called out, not waiting for a reply as he went looking for the stationmaster.

Reg kept up a steady pace onto the iron bridge and along the line as it swung out of sight around the back of the hall.

9

Zillah walked back in the direction of Waratah, towards the tiny figure coming into view. They met halfway along the straight and Reg kissed her on the cheek, gesturing for them to cross into the paddock. She could swear there was alcohol on his breath but it was too early in the day for that so she decided it was probably Listerine. Yes, definitely mouthwash.

The pressure in her stomach was a heavy hand squeezing under her rib cage. What was he going to say? She hoped it wouldn't take too long or Kathleen would be waiting back at the gate, cursing her and getting wound up. Then it would be hell to pay getting her to calm down again.

Zillah knew how it worked with Reg, though. Mostly he needed time, slow-spooling like the reels of film that came to town, unwinding into what he wanted to say. She could handle Kathleen in a fit of temper because she'd done it before. The stronger pull was to what Reg might have by way of a flimsy option.

He led them towards the edge of the paddock, to a clearing marked out on three sides by fallen logs from a forest that had once covered the area now used occasionally to graze cattle. Nearby, a few stubborn stands of scrub remained. Though the cattle had moved on to less exposed pastures for the approaching winter, a line of broken twiggy branches at the height of their shoulders showed where they had pushed in for shelter in previous seasons.

"Let's sit for a bit. I thought we could have a fare-well drink, it might be the last chance we get," he said, shifting the paper bag from one arm to the other with the sound of glass clinking.

This was not what Zillah had expected, especially when Reg knew she wasn't much of a one for drink-ing, but there was such gravity in the moment that she held back any questions or protest. If this was what he needed to speak his mind, she would go along with it.

The grass was still damp from the dew so she took off her coat and spread it on the ground for them, sitting to one side while he settled beside her. The warmth of his arm around her shoulders felt good and he gave her a squeeze as he stretched his legs out beside hers.

"You know, you mean the world to me," he said, loosening his tie, his eyes directed to his feet.

A flock of yellow-tailed black cockatoos flapped slowly by and landed in a nearby pine tree, where they began squealing and ripping into the cones with their hooked beaks. Chunks of cones rained down on the ground: thunk, thunk, thunk. The lookout bird gave one long squawk and they all lifted their heads and looked south. Whatever it had heard didn't trouble them for long and they resumed their noisy feeding.

Soon after, for no apparent reason, they rose together and taking their ruckus with them, flew off in the direction of the mountain.

The couple on the coat sat quietly for a while in the companionship of not knowing what should come next. But Reg sensed if he left it too long to say what was needed, she might get anxious about her friend and decide she had to leave.

"Zillah, I haven't said it before but I love you and I know you care about me." He was jabbering now, the words tumbling fast, and he needed to crank his speech back to a more soothing pace. "It breaks my heart to think we could part."

She was looking at him, at all the pain in his eyes, just like the night he'd proposed. She wanted so badly to console him, to make it all right but as she searched for kind words, her guilt was rising up to meet him and a great fog dulled her mind.

The ground was cold through her coat and she wrapped her arms around her knees, her chin resting there. Her eyes settled on her chipped nails. They were tiny, broken trophies in their own way, she thought, signs of success if the measure of victory was in hard work. She smiled ruefully at Reg and he flashed a tight grin in return.

In the distance, they heard the Magnet train pull in and men shouting in a friendly fashion above the work of transferring the load to the wagons bound for Burnie. They were sounds familiar to Zillah from the time she'd been old enough to wander outside but today it was an orchestra of industry, with its own music in the rise and fall, sharp and flat, the clipped notes flying high and others stretching low. She thought better about mentioning it to Reg and watched as he reached over to his left, a little behind him, where he'd placed the bag. It was a small reprieve, enough to give her the chance to find something worthwhile and comforting to say to him.

"You know I care about you. I want us to go on, Reg. You leaving doesn't mean it's the end. We just have to stay positive and keep believing we can find a way." Even to her, her words sounded thin and use-less. The conflict of their situation was getting harder and all the avoiding she'd been doing had, it turned out, been no help at all.

As she berated herself, keeping her eyes from his by watching a long streak of cloud dissolve near the horizon, he pulled out the beer and balanced it care-fully on the grass while he reached in the bag for the bottle opener and the nip glass.

She was pleased to see, as he handed her the glass, that he'd only half-filled it and she wouldn't have to make it even harder for him by refusing to drink all the beer. He raised the bottle and tapped it against her glass.

"Cheers, darling girl."

He guzzled from the bottle while she took a sip.

The beer was far more bitter than she expected but she managed to stop herself from shuddering. The effect was a little like the assault of the bitter gooseberry skins on membranes in the mouth and you got used to them after a while. She wondered what Kathleen would think when she showed up with beer on her breath but quickly pushed the thought away.

"I'm just so sorry it's been difficult, Reg," she whispered.

She took another sip and nuzzled in towards him. He leaned down and kissed her on the forehead, tender and deliberate.

"Drink up, my girl, it's all going to be alright."

He gulped a mouthful of beer, practised at balancing the tall bottle so it poured at the right pace, and waited while she drank again from the glass. The alcohol was loosening her tongue.

"We could have been married by now if it wasn't for religion and I could have been leaving with you on Saturday."

A single tear ran down the side of her nose and he brushed it away, crooning soft sounds in her ear before she had the chance to say how awful it was that he was leaving or worse, to blurt out how unbearable it was that he might be taking with him her only chance of a future. She was crying now and he reached in his pants pocket and pulled out a folded handkerchief, pressing it into her hand.

"There's no need to be upset, really no need at all," he said softly. He loosened his tie, pulling it off and throwing it down beside him.

He seemed so confident that she dried her eyes and was quiet. He put his arm back around her and hugged her tight.

"You and I, we are going to be together forever."

It was absolute, the way he said it, and her skin, muscle and bone gently fused, melting and giddy in the idea of being loved always. A man who wanted her, who held her so entirely, made her dizzy with his touch; who was so sure. He was certain and, in the dissolving of chest and limbs, a word sprang up, a pinprick of irritation. *I will not pay attention, I am not listening.*

The wanting was burning, a bright nebula spinning forward into the light through the grey fog. But the centre collapsed and there was no hot star, just the swirling and turning.

She put one hand on the ground to steady her and pulled back a little to look at him. "What do you mean?"

She was floating, aware of Reg and the paddock and her coat beneath them, yet not feeling the contact with the ground or his solid shoulder. Her belly tightened as she registered the unfamiliar tone in the way he spoke, a look on his face that seemed to surround her, swallow her up. She was struggling to make sense of it.

"I mean we will always be together. Nothing is ever going to come between us again."

His words were as fervent as Father Hayes' at the pulpit when he was in full flight. She didn't understand what Reg said. She was listening carefully but he wasn't making sense and a sick, anxious wave began to surge within her. She had almost finished the beer and sat the glass down, taking his hand in hers.

"Reg, I don't know what you're saying. Is there something on your mind that you're not telling me?" The fog had burned off, she was direct with him this time. Perhaps it hadn't been such a good idea to meet him and be alone here when he was clearly getting into a state.

"You and I, we're going to go together."

She turned her head to the left, looking straight at him. With eyes wide, she watched his mouth move and captured the string of words in an instant. Her mind the simple shutter on a Box Brownie, she didn't need a tray of chemicals to process what it caught. A picture, focused and clear, hung there in the light on his face, the shadow of his pupils, the fall of his mouth.

She lunged across him and grabbed the paper bag, dragged it onto her lap and thrust her hand inside to pull out the remaining contents. In her open palm was a small brown bottle. She knew what it was. There was one just like it up high on a shelf in the woodshed at home.

"What have you done? What have you done?"

A terrible wailing was in her ear, on and on, and at first she didn't recognise the shrill pitch as her own. She wanted to hit him, tear at his hair. She wanted to scream, to get up and run and keep on running and find cheerful Kathleen or propel herself the other way back to her mother and the wonderful ordinariness of washing day. But she was dry and empty, a beetle husk pinned to the spot.

He was holding her, kissing her face, laying her gently down on the coat.

"Shhhh, I'm here, it's okay my darling girl. It's all okay."

She had seen her father baiting carrots for the rabbits, shaking out the tiny colourless crystals to make a paste with bicarbonate and laundry starch. She had watched how they dissolve almost instantly. She imagined Reg stopping on the side of the railway line and tipping a few crystals into the glass before coming to meet her.

She moaned and tossed her head from side to side. "You can't do this, you mustn't do this, it's a mortal sin." She saw her arms flailing and his face above hers, concerned and steady.

"I'm here, I'm looking after you," he whispered over and over, stroking her cheek as the sky spun above her and she travelled across it, searching its immensity. But it offered no deliverance.

Soon after, she shuddered once and went limp in his arms. He had been bracing himself for the horror of the poison-induced convulsions. Determined to keep his resolve and do all he could to ease her through it, to give her all the love he could as she travelled ahead to heaven or hell. He didn't know which but, wherever it was, she would be waiting for him.

He hadn't counted on her going so quickly. Inexplicably, below what he could see in skin and bones at her throat, her thyroid had reacted immediately and viciously, the toxicity of the strychnine and the shock of taking the poison slamming it into overdrive. It erupted in a cardiac arrest.

He checked for a pulse and when he found none, flung himself down on her chest, shaking and rigid. His tongue was outside his control and the sounds that came first struck a logjam in his throat, exiting in a rough keening that stalled then restarted, stuttering cries muffled by her hair. It was done. It was done and it hurt more than he could ever have expected.

Reg lay with her for a long time, lost in her smell and the softness of her face, his mind emptied out by the crying and the ache so tight across his ribs he could only manage half-breaths. At some point in the afternoon he reached for her hand and it was cool, and he saw that she was no longer there.

As he returned to the reality of what needed to

come next, he pushed up into a sitting position. Christ, what an effort to sit upright and pull his mind back from the cave in the back of his skull. He looked around on the ground. Where was it? His arm acted independently, without instruction from his brain, reaching for the small bottle before he'd recognised what it was.

He unscrewed the cap and, fumbling, jerked a few crystals into the glass then poured in some beer and watched the poison cloud in the flat ale then disappear completely. He raised the glass to his mouth but thought better of it and sat it down beside him on the coat. It could not be like this.

In the inside pocket of his jacket he found a stub of pencil. He plucked at the paper bag, where it had been wedged under her hip. He flattened out the creases as best he could. He needed to write something, to let them know it was okay, that they were okay. He leaned into it, his elbow digging into his thigh to steady the hand. You can do it, he told himself. You can.

He focused with what he had left, slowly printing in neat, masculine handwriting, the letters careful. One word was it, all he could manage. *Goodbye*. He lay the bag down beside him and placed the pencil on top to hold it down. At that precise moment, adrenaline kicked in.

He emptied the contents of the glass down his

throat in one swift action then snatched at the poison bottle and swung his arm wide to toss it as far away as he could. He scanned the scene for the first time, smoothing out the coat, straightening the wrinkle in one of her socks. He tried to close her eyes but the lids were already stiff and she stared endlessly at the sky.

Rest, my sweetheart. It's time to rest.

He picked up the handkerchief she'd discarded and shook it out, kissing her one last time before laying the checked cotton square from her hairline to her chin in a graceful movement he'd seen the reverend make as he passed the water down the face of a baby at the christening font.

With great care, he stretched out her left arm to form an arc and laid his head there, though it was unyielding without her heat. His left arm curled across her waist and he lifted his knee so it gently rested on her leg. He knew that, unlike her, it would probably go for hours; that he would not be spared. And he knew, too, that he didn't deserve to be. He waited for it to start.

Back at Magnet Junction, after an hour of waiting and looking down the railway line, Kathleen had given up on Zillah and gone blackberry picking with her brother, towards the nearby reservoir and away from Delphin's Paddock.

Late in the afternoon at the Camp Road house, darkness fell and the evening meal was its usual bustling affair. It wasn't until about nine o'clock that Alice started to feel on edge about Zillah. Although she often visited friends or stayed overnight, she was a responsible girl and it wasn't like her to be more than two hours past the time she would normally be home.

By half past nine, the agitation had turned to anxiety and Alice decided she couldn't wait any longer. She sent Isobel to the police station to report that Zillah was missing. When Isobel banged on the door of the first police house with lights on, it was Constable Donovan who opened it.

10

Michael Donovan was no fool. After leaving school he'd stayed on in the Westbury district as a farmhand for five or so years before joining the force, and it was deep in him, the Catholic code hammered into the roots of his and other Irish families. Everything not-Catholic was a threat to the values that kept their families bound one to the other, including his own; the values that made them who they were, separating them from evil forces and making their suffering holy and worthwhile.

He had married before his original posting to Waratah and although their first baby had been born and died in Hobart just five months after the wedding, his wife was still a good Catholic. Here at Waratah, they had made a fresh start and a new family.

He'd seen Zillah and Reg at the dances. He had known the risk she was taking and, once or twice, when he'd passed her in the main street, had wanted to ask if she understood the trouble it might lead to. But it wasn't police business and he'd left it alone.

Now it was his business and it was urgent. He immediately went to the Bischoff Hotel, where Cyril confirmed that Reg's bed was empty.

Zillah's older brothers, Reg's roommate, Kathleen's father and a few others who could be roused from warm beds searched in the dark, continuing till well after midnight at which time Constable Donovan called it off till daylight. Soon after dawn, they gathered again behind the hall where he'd last seen Reg and the men followed the railway line towards the junction with the Magnet tramway, fanning out in a search pattern on either side.

Though it wasn't said aloud, most believed the pair had run off together and were not unduly concerned. Donovan didn't let on that he had searched Reg's room and all his clothes were still there or that he'd sworn Cyril to secrecy for now because he wasn't sure what it meant.

Alice had spent the morning steeling herself for the shock and the shame of a runaway daughter, which was the only possible explanation for Zillah treating Kathleen so badly, let alone her own flesh and blood. A thousand times, she went over what she would say when she got Zillah back. They were harsh words, cutting words, because the girl needed to know she'd done wrong and it might even take a sharp slap for her to get the message that it wasn't down to her to be deciding such things and taking off like that.

She knew Zillah was keen on Reg Sutton, Isobel had hinted at it, but she didn't think it was serious. She should have kept her home more, kept her close instead of letting her roam the town but she'd been such a good girl, one she could count on.

When she heard the handle turn on the back door, she was still furious but couldn't deny the small wave of relief that came before she saw it was Bill and remembered one of the men had gone down to the camp to fetch him.

"Which direction's Donovan gone?" was all he said.

He looked smaller than usual, as she pointed in the direction of Magnet Junction and told him: "They're searching up the line towards the Kelly place".

He was out the door straight away. No comfort for her or a single gesture of support, just like all the other times. She could not say how long she stood looking at the door while the not knowing burrowed its way into her chest but eventually she straightened her shoulders and got busy making a big lunch for the men.

It had been nearly five hours and they had searched everywhere that Zillah and Reg had last been seen when Donovan told them to pack it in, announcing he would make inquiries elsewhere. The men knew what that probably meant and headed home or to work, ready to report there was a scandal brewing.

About 1.30 pm, local councillor Albert Langmaid buttoned up his best jacket and left home for the monthly meeting of the Waratah Municipal Council, where he represented the East Ward. Unlike others at Magnet Junction, Albert was a dairy farmer and although he was still milking twice a day, autumn would soon come to an end and the Friesians would dry off. The pleasing thought of an extra hour in bed in the mornings lightened his step as he walked towards the town.

About a quarter of a mile down the railway line towards Waratah, he stopped and shoved a boot on the bottom wire of the nearby fence while lifting the strand of barbed wire above it, stooping through the gap with great care to make sure he didn't get his pants caught. The short cut through the paddock towards the road was his satisfying little ritual, marking the simple pleasure of going out. As he skirted around some low undergrowth surrounding rotting logs pushed aside when the paddock had been cleared, he saw something out of place and remembered the earlier conversation with his neighbour Kelly about the missing girl.

He didn't need to get up close to see they were long gone, the girl stiff on her back, her face covered, and the distorted body of the man stretched across her. What a mess and now he knew where she'd been going the day before when he saw her hurrying down the railway line, full of life and purpose. He was half-running now and it seemed to take forever but it was really only fifteen minutes or so before he got to the police station.

Constable Donovan looked fit to lose his lunch

when Albert told him the news but the copper went straight for the keys to the old Harley Davidson police bike, gesturing for Albert to get in the sidecar so he could lead him to the site. The bike lurched forward, spokes spinning and tyres spitting loose gravel, and they roared and rattled through the town, leaving a few curious bystanders watching the bike's dusty trail heading towards the junction.

Ever a practical man, the councillor guided Donovan to the bodies then arranged to continue on to his meeting and go to the station afterwards to make a statement. The minutes of the Waratah Municipal Council recorded that Councillor Langmaid moved two motions that afternoon, the first endorsing the appointment of a new employee for sanitary work and grave-digging at award rates; and the second ensuring that the section of gravel from Magnet Junction Road to Camp Road be top-dressed at the first available opportunity.

He was speaking to the second motion when Donovan, in the Housego kitchen, threw an arm around Alice to steady her before she slumped into a chair, a scream never making it from her throat. All the imagining Alice had done since sending Isobel to the constable had not gone anywhere near the possibility of a lover's death pact. She had not for a second expected that.

A week or more later, the *Truth* newspaper, from

the safe distance of Brisbane, would speculate that: "A feature of the case is the entire absence of a concrete theory as to the possible cause of the tragedy". From her chair, the air knocked from her lungs, all Alice could say in an endless loop was that Zillah was such a cheerful girl and never in trouble and there was no reason why she would take her own life. Next to her, Jean was crying in the messy, spontaneous way of the young, sobbing as much because her mother's torment was disturbing as she was because they were saying her fun-loving sister was never coming back.

Her father and brothers were spared the sight of Zillah's empty face when Donovan, who had known her for years, offered to do the formal identification. Allan was called on to identify Reg, arriving from Burnie to be taken to the morgue.

"When last I saw him, he was in his usual health and spirits. He made no complaint of any financial worries," he wrote in neat, thin lines on the witness deposition form for the coroner.

The formalities completed, the bodies were available for post-mortem examination by Dr Edwin Ick-Hewins, who had the misfortune to be doing a locum for the medical superintendent of the Mount Bischoff Provident Hospital and was therefore the responsible medical practitioner.

The doctor took his time setting up his tray and instruments. The routine was familiar but no matter how often he sliced open a body to reveal flesh, sinew and bone or remove organs, he could never extract the singularity of story that once had made a person. That weight sat heavily in his hands as he went about his work.

He examined Zillah's body first, noting it was that of a well-nourished girl in her early twenties. There were no external marks of violence and no indication of suffocation by strangling or otherwise. All the organs appeared to be normal until he came to the region of the throat and neck.

Reg's body showed a well-developed male in early manhood with an old scar on the left leg just below the groin and another about eight inches long on the left kneecap. "On opening the body, all organs appeared normal until I examined the lungs. They were very congested, the right one especially so and even the lining of the ribs on that side was greatly congested," he wrote later in his report.

A sergeant from Burnie was present during the autopsies and left with two sealed bottles, each containing a stomach, as well as the ale bottle, whisky glass and small brown bottle, all bound for the government analyst's laboratory in Hobart.

Dr Ick-Hewins' initial findings were not released till the coronial inquiry opened Friday morning but were hinted at in the two funeral notices printed one above the other in the newspaper. The headline on an earlier page pronounced "Suicide Pact Indicated", yet the funeral details suggested something else.

Zillah's coffin left her parents' residence after lunch, followed by seven carloads of her friends, and was taken to the Star of the Sea Catholic Church at Burnie for a 4 pm service, then on for burial at the Wivenhoe cemetery. Her father and brothers were listed as the chief mourners but, scarcely able to bear the burden of her death, they left it to the Randall cousins to shoulder the coffin on its journey from church to hearse then grave.

There was no mention of church for Reg's funeral the next day. His body was taken from the Wilmot Street cottage to the same cemetery, where a large gathering of footballers from Waratah and Burnie, surf-lifesavers and family friends stood in subdued fashion alongside Alice, sisters Lucy and Winnie and brothers Horrie, Allan, Owen and Cliff and the mound of wreaths on the opposite side of the open grave.

ON THE FRIDAY, BEFORE the pair had been buried, Allan Sutton's statement identifying his brother was provided to district coroner, Christian Stitz. Then Constable Donovan took the oath and confirmed that he had identified Zillah, before outlining the circumstances of the case. He was cautious with his words and specific, as any professional officer of the law should be, but his final statement veered into the territory of the testimonial: "I saw the deceased two or three days before her death. I have known her for approximately seven years. She always appeared to me to be a cheerful, bright girl. She was in no difficulties as far as I know. I never received any complaints about her."

Dr Ick-Hewins was then sworn in and gave his initial evidence, describing the relaxed, perfect composure of Zillah's limbs and features and the healthy condition of her organs, except for a large growth at the throat. He had found, according to his account, the likely cause for the sudden heart failure that led to a peaceful death.

"I discovered a goitrous swelling of the thyroid gland, the greater part of which was well buried in the neck. The right lobe was twice as large as the left and was about four inches long by two inches wide and an inch thick. The lower end of both right and left lobes showed evidence of congestion," he told the coroner.

Reg's body, however, showed straining on the face and down the front, with some bleeding from the mouth, and the muscles of the calves were drawn up in knots, all indicative of death as a result of ingesting strychnine. "Everything that I saw both externally and internally pointed to death having taken place as the result of the ingestion of such a poison as strychnine."

The doctor was blunt in describing both deaths though more delicate about another matter. "The girl led a chaste life," he told the coroner.

While analysis would determine if the girl's stomach did or did not contain strychnine, "it is my opinion that death occurred suddenly from heart failure brought on by sudden excessive action of the thyroid gland, stimulated by fear or shock, which shock may have been caused or intensified by drinking an irritant poison".

Three weeks later, the inquiry reconvened to hear from the final witnesses, including Zillah's mother: "I had no idea she was going to meet Sutton that morning. My daughter had been going with the deceased for about eight or nine months." Alice stiffened and looked up from the statement signed with a shaky hand, before continuing.

"She never told me that he proposed to marry her. I don't think I would have approved of her marrying Sutton. Zillah was a very cheerful girl and she was in her usual spirits on the morning she left to go blackberry picking."

The chemist, Ernest West, was next. "I knew the deceased, Reginald Sutton. I have known him for a period of years." Yes, he had required him to leave the shop and locate a witness and had obtained both signatures, in accordance with the Pharmaceutical Act, before he sold the strychnine. Only the sergeant was close enough to catch the tremble in the chemist's hand as he produced the register showing the date of the sale, the deceased's address and occupation, the purpose for which the poison was required, "killing rabbits", and the signatures of the two men.

Cyril Alexander began with the basics: "I am a bartender at Waratah and I have known the deceased Reginald Colin Sutton all my life. He was occupying a room at the Bischoff Hotel with me on and off for about ten days prior to his death."

The coroner, however, was more interested in final events and Cyril was questioned at length about the twenty-four hours at the hotel before the deaths.

"The last night he was in the room, I went to bed at eleven o'clock and Sutton was in bed then and was asleep. I had no conversation with him."

The barman talked through the sequence on the final morning, the pair having breakfast, Reg slipping out to the kitchen to wipe up the breakfast dishes, then returning to the bar.

"When he purchased the bottle of ale, Sutton appeared in his usual good spirits," Cyril said. He neither offered nor was asked for an opinion on the quantity of alcohol Reg has consumed before leaving the hotel.

Sergeant Butler presented the report from the government analyst. Both stomachs contained strychnine. The coroner recalled Dr Ick-Hewins to respond to the new information but Ick-Hewins was not swayed.

"Although strychnine was found in Miss Housego's organs, I am still of the opinion that she died from heart failure caused by the sudden shock of taking poison, either willingly or unwillingly."

Christian Stitz announced a short adjournment, retreating to a small office at the rear of the building, where he sat alone and reviewed his notes. He had conducted coronial inquiries in mining towns the length of the West Coast and was familiar with the best of human nature and its underbelly. From where he sat, death wore many faces: a mine rockfall, house fire, sinking boat or a rearing horse. Sometimes it was a husband who beat his unhappy wife into oblivion or a brother unskilled with a shotgun yet able to blow out the brain of his sibling just the same. This was his first encounter with death in a small, brown bottle.

He resumed the hearing about twenty minutes later, the clerk calling the courtroom to order. After outlining a brief summary of the evidence, he gave his finding. He concluded that Reg came by his death through strychnine poisoning at his own hand. Then he returned an open finding on Zillah's death.

At the back of the Waratah courthouse, Kathleen had defied her father to stay on after giving her evidence earlier in the day. As the coroner spoke, she burst into tears and covered her eyes with one hand but before she could get the other one to her mouth, she was whimpering. She was led out of the courthouse, bent over and supported on either side.

It had taken Constable Donovan a while to track her down, late the evening that the bodies had been removed from Delphin's Paddock to the mortuary. The poor kid was still in shock, rubbing one arm then the next as though she could wipe away the events of the day. Her mother leaned over and put another log on the fire but stayed close by.

Donovan, not wanting to intimidate Kathleen, removed his tall helmet and placed it on the table. As he did, firelight flashed on his helmet badge, making his identity number of 920 pulse and dance. Out of habit, he ran one hand through his hair in a futile attempt to remove the flattened circle made by the helmet band.

As he asked careful questions and recorded the answers verbatim in his black notebook, Kathleen pieced together what she knew, starting with the night she and Zillah had met Reg at the hall. Now and then she lapsed into commentary, as though she was trying to work things out for herself as much as she wanted to help the policeman.

"He was good to Zillah, he seemed to think a lot of her."

Donovan was going slower than he had with the others; she seemed more fragile, less capable of keeping it together. They got to the part where Zillah had met her at the gate, leaving the bucket and billy.

"It was the last time I saw her alive. She seemed quite normal and happy," Kathleen stuttered, the tears starting up again.

She told them how Zillah had shared the news about a month earlier that Reg had proposed but that she'd told him she couldn't marry without the consent of her mother. By the time Kathleen got to the moment where she had taken a final look down the railway line at noon to see if Zillah was there, Donovan was ready to leave, drained from wading through the grief of others while, below the shiny buttons on his jacket, he was struggling with his own festering sorrow.

Kathleen quieted and the constable nodded in her mother's direction to indicate he was taking his leave. He'd just closed the notebook and was putting the pen in his top pocket when the girl jolted forward, clapping both hands over her mouth. Donovan and Mary Kelly both jumped, the girl's alarm filling the space between them.

She was babbling then, words pouring out but in no particular order and he was relieved when Mrs Kelly leaned over with a firm touch on the girl's shoulder. He was so utterly tired and beyond the ability to deal with any hysterics.

"I think I should go, thanks Mrs Kelly."

But Kathleen grabbed his jacket cuff and a stream of words kept coming, the girl's voice stammering at first then rushing forward.

"I remember, I remember it now, it's come back, Tuesday night when she got back to her mother's after meeting Reg and I was waiting in the bed and already falling asleep and she was talking to me and telling me things and I was trying to keep awake and listen but I went to sleep and when I woke up next morning I'd forgotten but I remember now and I've been trying to get it back all week and it's been just out of reach."

Mrs Kelly leaned down so her face was in front of Kathleen's and held up a broad hand. "Kathleen, me darlin', it's not making a lot of sense. Now take a big breath and tell the constable clear as you can what it is you've remembered."

The girl's chest heaved in then out. When she spoke, her voice came from a deeper place than before.

"Zillah was telling me something important and at the time I knew it was really important and I should remember, but it slipped away because I was so sleepy. And now it's come back.

"She told me that night that she and Reg had had words while they were walking, that they had fought over her not being willing to marry him." Kathleen paused and lifted her head to look directly at the constable.

"She told me he had said that if he could not get her, then no-one else would."

Donovan was done; he had to get out of there.

Before Mrs Kelly had finished closing the front door, he was on the bike with the headlights on and the loud whumping of the engine was shattering the still night, making sure there was no chance to hear any more. He was angry now, with the whole damn lot of them, especially himself. As the bike growled and rattled down the road, he banged his fist hard on the metal panel of the sidecar, glad to feel the knuckles sting.

They had all been looking on in their own way over the months: Reg's brother, his mates, Zillah's family, her friends, but not one of them had eyes to see. He had been trained to observe and yet he was as bad as the rest of them.

Blind, the whole lot of them, to what was being set up behind the curtain, even as it began drawing back over recent weeks. They didn't need a damn ticket because they had a front row seat. They would all have to live with it because it could not be undone; there was no way to make another ending.

As he drove from the junction and spun the Harley left onto the main road, the first frost for the year was already forming in the dark. Tiny ice crystals were settling on the roadside, stealing across the grass and clinging to tight clods of soil kicked up by Reg's boots in the nearby paddock.

Author's Note

Zillah was my aunt and although I was born long after she had gone, the space where once she had been remained a deep, silent wound in the family. I never once heard my father Phil—Zillah's brother—bring himself to say her name.

It was years before I knew she'd even existed and several more after that before my mother, Frances, in response to my questioning, indicated her death had not been straightforward. As a girl, mum had been a friend of Zillah's youngest sister, Jean, and she had seen the family's awful pain first-hand.

No doubt Reg's death profoundly affected his family also.

I have remained true, insofar as possible, to the facts in original depositions to the coronial inquiry; as well as information in newspaper articles of the day about circumstances surrounding the two deaths and relating to incidents involving key individuals; prison and military records; historical accounts and published local histories.

However, while the dialogue and inferences about purpose or motivation draw heavily on the research, they are entirely fictional.

Printed in Great Britain
by Amazon

17667572R00108